BRICK OF SOUND 2

BY

MADISON PATE

BRICK OF SOUND 2
BY
MADISON PATE

T&J PUBLISHERS
A SMALL INDEPENDENT PUBLISHER WITH A BIG VOICE

Printed in the United States of America by
T&J Publishers (Atlanta, GA.)
www.TandJPublishers.com

Cover design by Supply Graphics
Book format and layout by Timothy Flemming, Jr. (T&J Publishers)

ISBN: 978-1-7360003-1-1

To contact author, go to:

Website: www.madison-pate.com
Email: contact@madison-pate.com
Facebook: Madison Pate
Instagram: Brick of Sound
LinkedIn: Madison Pate

This book is dedicated to my band teacher Mr. Carr. Thank you for teaching me more about music and helping me in general.

TABLE OF CONTENTS

CHLOE WALKED INTO THE DOOR OF THE BAND House. It was now May, and she had finished the training she did in a cave. She just mediated to be able to negate EP Allie's mind control. Mandy went up to her.

"You're right on time. We're having a meeting now." She told her, walking off. Chloe followed her towards the room that she was heading towards.

"This is crazy, you guys!" Ms. Martinez shouted at them. Brandon was fiddling around with a pen that he had found the day before. Chloe sat down in a chair, then with Mandy following next.

"We've been planning this for months. It's gonna work." Mandy responded. Chloe thought of an idea.

"I mean, don't you guys know that if 345 is separated from Madison for too long, she could die?" Chloe asked.

"Exactly! The time that she can live is 2 months! It's been almost 2 months already, that's why we should use the plan now!" Mandy said. Ms. Martinez thought about this for a minute or two

"Alright, fine. I'll let you guys do it. But, if you fail at this, you're all banned from band!" Ms. Martinez finished, then walking out the door.

In the Villain Hideout

Madison was tied to a chair, with heavy weights around her hands, so she wouldn't be able to use Power. EP Allie walked up to her.

"You still think you're strong? Just look at yourself! You're weak." EP Allie said to her. Madison looked up at her.

"I'm still way stronger than you." Madison retaliated, causing EP Allie to begin charging up energy. She blasted her at point blank range, which would have normally killed her in the state she was in, but it barely did any damage.

"I told you so, idiot." EP Allie backed up a bit.

"You're going to die soon anyway." She said, then walking off. Madison looked back down at the ground.

"She thinks that I don't even know that."

At the Kelli Squad base

"You guys can go ahead and start your part of the plan." Mandy said, over a phone. They all began putting on equipment that would help them throughout the mission.

"Let's show them that we're super strong!" Kelli exclaimed, putting on her signature goggles.

CHAPTER 1: RESCUE MISSION

In a forest near the Villain Hideout

"I'm going to get my student back!" Ms. Martinez called out, releasing a bunch of energy from her superiority. 345 Madison teleported to where she was.

"You wish." 345 Madison responded, firing off energy from the curse towards her. Ms. Martinez jumped to dodge the attack.

"Sorry, but I'm not your opponent!" She said, vanishing, leaving a bunch of sun energy behind. Brandon appeared from behind the energy, making it disperse with the wind force from Impact.

"Rocket Punch!" He shouted, charging towards her, using the rocket superiority at his feet. He reeled back a fist, and tried to punch 345 Madison.

"Dark Shot!" 345 Madison yelled, shooting a wave of energy towards him. This didn't affect him.

"Bring it on, idiot!" Brandon used an impact like attack to push himself towards the curse. 345 Madison used a cursed blast to try and push him away, but he dodged any blasts that came his way, even while being immune to it.

"Alright then, you can actually prove a fight."

Back in the Villain Hideout

EP Allie was outside of the hideout, seeming to be waiting for something. Ms. Martinez appeared, charging an attack.

"The fake hero has arrived!" EP Allie taunted. Ms. Martinez teleported above her and fired off a large blast with her hand alone.

"Amazing Impact!" She shouted, adding more energy to the blast. Meanwhile, in the inside of the hideout, the Kelli Squad walked in. Madison looked at them.

"My favorite squad is here to save me?" Madison asked them. Aaliyah used her power, which was Gravity, a Sub-Legendary, to remove the weights from her arms. Kelli removed the Power chains that were keeping Madison stuck to the chair, and then gave her a high five.

"Of course we are!" Kelli answered. Madison noticed how weak she looked, since she was hit by blasts basically every day for two months. Maybe it was also caused by how Power World was basically almost crumbled into pieces, but she didn't know for sure.

They brought her outside, for her to see EP Allie knocked out by Ms. Martinez. Madison waved towards her.

"Ms. Martinez!" She yelled in excitement, something that she hadn't had in months now.

"It's nice to see you again!" She responded, then using sun energy to vanish back to the band house. Chloe appeared with Mandy on her back, and dropping her on the ground. She began walking towards Madison.

"What's up, Mandy?" Madison asked her. Mandy punched Madison in the stomach, right where the seal was.

"You've got some nerve." Madison held on to her shirt, before falling over Mandy's shoulder.

"Just shut up for one more moment." She said, then walking over to Chloe. They then began flying off back to the band house.

As they arrived at the band house, Madison had soon woken up after being knocked out. Once Mandy landed, Chloe had flown off to somewhere else, leaving the two of them there.

"I thought I told you to not come back for me." Madison said, trying to muster up the Power that was still left in her.

"You would've eventually died if we didn't come for you!" Mandy responded.

"Do you think I don't know that? I was fully prepared for this, and you guys decided to interrupt that!" Madison shouted towards her, which somewhat caught her off guard.

"Everything that's happened, it's all my fault! Epitomus Madison dying, Ms. Martinez getting kidnapped, and everything else!" She continued.

"Every time I tried to not think about it, it always came back! I don't want to be a weakling who can't function!"

"I'm not even a true hero anymore!" She finished.

Mandy charged a small flame in her hand.

"A true hero is respected by everyone! How do you think we feel? You've become so selfish!" Mandy yelled, firing it towards Madison, who didn't even try to block it. The attack did virtually nothing. Madison charged towards Mandy, and fired off a large blast.

"You guys don't care. Even while trapped in that chair, she tortured me with all of these things that were happening!" Mandy grabbed her by her arm and slammed her on the ground, which caused her to cough up blood. Madison got up and charged up an energy enhanced punch.

"How do you think I feel?" She asked, punching her straight in the face. Mandy grabbed her arm again, and because of how weak she was at the moment, managed to throw her up into the air.

"Like an idiot!" Mandy flew upwards to where Madison was, and used a sledgehammer like attack to send her flying down to the ground. Madison slammed into the ground, but then got up soon after. She waited for Mandy to come closer to where she was.

"Powerful Takedown!" Madison shouted, punching her in the face, and then grabbing her by the face, firing off multiple blasts until she reached the ground, when she fired off a very large blast which made her lose all of the energy left in her.

"That's for tomo-" She said, then being hit by an Erasure attack from Ms. Martinez, which knocked her out.

"She has to wait until the curse returns to her body if she wants to fight anyone again."

CHAPTER 2: TRUE HERE?

Back in the forest near the Villain Hideout

Brandon was still fighting 345 Madison, as there was a big power difference, but he still could stand strong. She charged up a large ball of dark energy.

"This is Madison's pain at the moment." 345 Madison told him. He had his arms crossed.

"If you take this pain, I'll return back to her body." Brandon walked towards the energy.

"That's a deal." He said, then putting both of his hands into it, which caused a very large explosion, which leveled the entire forest.

At the Villain Hideout

Chloe dropped down to the Hideout, to see EP Allie still knocked out.

"Just how strong is Ms. Martinez?" She thought, then looking over to the Kelli Squad.

"Extra Crispy!" Kandi shouted, and everyone but Kelli agreed.

"...What are they even talking about?" She asked herself, then looking at Chloe.

"Good job guys on getting Madison back!" Chloe said to them.

"Can we go to the band house and celebrate after we finish watching Epitomus Allie?" Kelli questioned her, and Chloe nodded. She then heard the large explosion from the forest, and then flew over there.

When she arrived, all she saw were destroyed trees. Chloe kept on looking around for Brandon. When she finally found him, he saw that he was completely battle damaged, and on the verge of dying, but still standing.

"Brandon! What the heck happened here?" She asked him, getting closer. He kept his arms crossed.

"Nothing." Chloe grabbed him by his shoulder, which ended up freezing her hand.

"It's obvious that something happened! That blast would've wiped out a few mountains, and now even your own body could freeze you to death!"

"I told you it's nothing…" He choked out, before completely blanking out. He still stood tall, though. But even the power of the strongest Sub-Legendary could not handle it.

"You think you can handle all of this, do you? It's way too early for you to die." Chloe mumbled, watching him slowly stumble, until falling. She caught him, and began picking him up.

"There's just too much to live for."

Back at the Band House

It had oddly started raining. Madison sat on a rock near the entrance, seeming to be thinking about something. Mandy looked at her while she was thinking.

"I told you already, I don't want to come back. I've already brought enough pain to you guys." Madison stated.

"Everyone misses you." Mandy responded. Madison looked back up to her, stopping her thought process.

"Do you?" She asked.

"No." Ms. Martinez had a death stare on her, so she decided to say something different.

"Yeah, I guess." She told her. The Kelli Squad arrived at the entrance, along with Chloe carrying the now unconscious Brandon.

"Those are your only reasons?" Madison asked Mandy. She nodded. Madison held her hand up to her face and fired off a small blast, which was weaker than the ones she usually did.

"You guys really do suck."

BRICK OF SOUND

MADISON'S POWER HAD BEEN COMING BACK TO her, so she decided to walk out of the band house and stand on a nearby tall rock. As 345 started coming back, the ground began shaking, because of how strong the curse is. She screamed very loudly, which caused an aura to rapidly surround her. It let out a large explosion, which ended up breaking the rock.

"Power World's coming back!" She exclaimed, jumping off the rock that was now half broken. Chloe walked out of the band house, and saw Madison.

"There's supposed to be a new recruit coming here soon." Chloe said, and Madison became happy.

"Oh! I know who it is!" Madison responded. She fired off multiple blasts, and they seemed to be in more shape than the day before.

"But, before you see them, you have a mission to do." Chloe finished, causing Madison to sort of lose the excitement.

"Really? This has to be good." She said, then crossing her arms.

"You have to fight against the Kelli Squad, and prove yourself that you're still strong!" Chloe shouted, pointing over to the direction that their base was.

"Woah! Do they have a base now?" Madison asked, now completely interested. Chloe nodded in response. She charged up Power at the bottom of her feet and launched herself towards the base.

Madison landed at the front of the base, to see the whole squad in the same equipment they had the day before.

"I'll go easy on you guys, even if I'm still weaker than usual." She told them, charging a small blast in her right hand. Kelli stepped up to fight her first.

"I'll fight you first!" She responded, launching a wave of water towards Madison. She used the small blast to propel herself upwards. Kandi appeared behind her, with the help of Aaliyah's gravity. Madison turned around to face her, as she was charging a blast of flames similar to Mandy's, but they were of the darker color.

"Mandy must've told you about Power's weakness!" She claimed, raising her arms to block the oncoming blast. Walter froze the time around Madison, so Kelli could send a barrage of water towards her. Both blasts connected to her.

"Shouldn't you kick it up a notch?" Kelli asked her, which was basically a taunt. Madison appeared on a nearby tree trunk, and had a bunch of smoke coming off of her. It seemed like their efforts didn't do anything.

"Well, maybe if all of you charged me, I would." She responded, not expecting the attack from above.

"Crossette!" Enza shouted, firing off a firework from her hand which constantly set off multiple other explosions.

"Good job!" Walter called out to Enza. Madison appeared on the top of the base, blowing away a fire that had caught onto her jacket.

"That was close." Madison said. She then sat down on the roof of the base, looking down to them.

"You guys have to try harder! Even Mandy before she got the blazes could beat you guys!" She told them. Then Kelli used water to shoot herself upwards, making her appear right in front of Madison.

"Take us seriously!" She shouted at her, causing Madison to get up. She pointed her hand towards her.

"Your loss!" She retaliated, firing off a large wave of energy, which sent her flying backwards. Aaliyah caught her with the gravity, and sent her flying towards Madison, which ended up hitting her.

"We finally got you!" Kandi proudly said. Madison backed up a bit, still on the roof. She charged up another blast, this time double-handed.

"You were so close to getting a good shot." Kandi and Enza both charged her at the same time. She used the blasts in an outward like explosion, which was around her, sending them back to their spot.

Walter caught Enza, and Aaliyah stopped Kandi from flying too far with the gravity, and dropped her down to the ground. Madison began stretching her arms.

"I'm just getting started!" She exclaimed, dropping off of the base, also hoping that she didn't damage it because she thought it was epic.

"The reason why I put you guys together, is because you all have prestige." She continued. They all were confused.

"Prestige is where after every battle, you get stronger. I have it too, but I thought an epic 5-person squad was cooler than 6!" Madison finished, firing off mini blasts from her hands. Kelli was the first person to speak.

"So, what does that mean?" Madison began spinning

in a circle, and flying up into the air. She charged two medi-um sized blasts in her hands.

"It means you guys are epic! Shiny Tornado!" She shouted, shooting towards them like a missile. Once she hit the ground, she fired off a very large blast, which engulfed the whole area, including the base.

"Good thing when I hold back, it doesn't cause any damage to the area around." Madison flew back to the band house using blasts. Once she landed, Chloe immediately came out.

"Bad news!" She exclaimed, grabbing Madison by her arm and dragging her into the band house. When they made it into the meeting room, she let go of Madison.

"Really? Now a sky island?" Mandy asked, complete-ly dumbfounded. Brandon said something incomprehensi-ble under his bandages, and she agreed.

"What is it now, Ms. Martinez?" Madison asked her, crossing her arms.

"So, Epitomus Allie just defeated a bunch of people on Caelum Insula. We have to save 2 specific people." Ms. Martinez answered her.

"Now she's somehow brought back the Epitomus versions of your friends, Karla and Kandace." Chloe contin-ued, and Ms. Martinez nodded.

"That's going to be a good story to tell." Madison stated. She then got a good question idea.

"Hey, uh, how are we going to get there?" She asked Ms. Martinez. She pointed out to the window, where the Epitomus ship was.

"That."

"Oh. Okay." Mandy began walking out the door, probably heading outside in advance.

"So, since those 3 still aren't here, I'll go get em' my-self." She claimed, surrounding her feet with flames, and boosting off.

Not even a full 5 minutes passed, and she returned with the 3 that she was talking about. It was Allie, Ashlyn, and Kendall, the new recruit that Chloe mentioned.

"Look, it's the short ones." Madison said, making fun of them somewhat.

"I'm taller than you." Ashlyn responded.

"That's beside the point."

"Oh wait! You guys got Madison back?" Allie asked them, and all of them nodded, except for Brandon, who had his reason.

"I'm here, aren't I?" Madison answered. Mandy hit her on the head, because of how stupid she thought her response was.

"Stop hitting me, you broken dust pan!" She retaliated, throwing 'Orange Juice Recipes' towards her.

"You started it, mop!" Mandy continued, launching it back to Madison. This went on for a few minutes until Chloe stopped them.

"Mandy, I know you're happy that Madison's back, but stop picking fights with her every five seconds!" She yelled at the both of them.

"Fine, I'm sorry." Ms. Martinez walked out the door.

"I'm going to go get the ship ready." She said. Madison fired off mini blasts again.

"Caelum Insula, here I come!"

BRICK OF SOUND

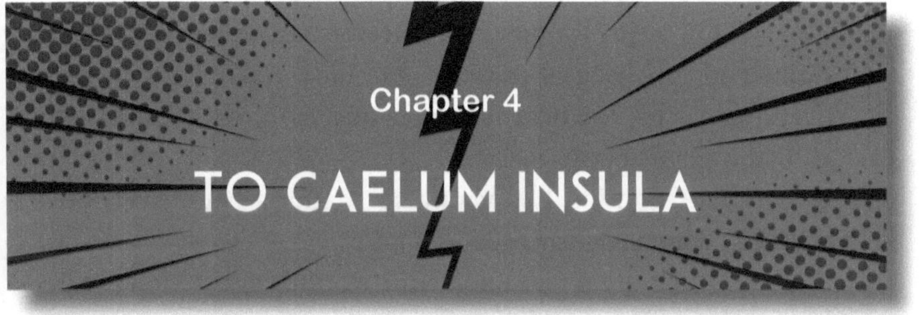

CHLOE WAS CHILLING IN HER ROOM ON THE SPACE-SHIP, w, minding her own business, until she heard a voice in her head.

"Section Leader!" The voice in her head shouted, and it sounded a lot like Madison's. She ran into Madison's room.

"What is it?" Chloe asked her. Madison was writing in 'Orange Juice Recipes'. She looked up to Chloe.

"I didn't say anything." Madison answered, leaving Chloe confused. She walked out of the room.

"Okay, that's good." She responded, walking back to her room. She began thinking.

"I'm going crazy or something. Maybe it's because Caelum Insula is the origin of Mythical powers." Chloe thought, opening the door to her room and sitting back down.

In the living room

"Once we land, I'm gonna chase her down." Mandy said to Kendall.

"I'm with you on that! I'm immortal, so I can follow you all the way there!" Kendall responded.

"Oh yeah, I forgot. Your powers are enhanced in the homeland of Mythical powers." Brandon walked out of his door, now with the band summer outfit on, with bandages still all over his body.

"I'm fighting her again, no matter what." Brandon claimed, which Mandy took as a joke.

"You'll die if you open your wounds again, don't you know that?" She asked him.

"Yeah, that applies to you too." He answered, sitting down in the chair across from the both of them. Chloe walked into the living room, and sat in a chair.

"Shut it, frosty." Mandy told Brandon.

"Not my fault that I wasn't told about 345 giving a curse, burnt food." He responded.

"Guys. Caelum has a gravity effect to it, that only affects non-Mythical users." Chloe said, causing both of them to change their focus on her.

"Are you serious? By how many times?" They both questioned her at the same time.

"10 times." Kendall and Chloe both started laughing at them. Madison came out of her room, now with the summer outfit on also.

"But it's 5 times for Legendary powers." Madison said, laughing. Even though it's only by a half, it barely affects her, because she's trained in this kind of gravity once before. Mandy threw a cup at her face, which ended up hitting her.

"Where do you get these cups from?" She angrily asked, running towards her. Mandy began running away.

"None of your business!" Madison caught up to her and locked her arms behind her back. Allie came out of her room, and sat down.

"Tell me!" Madison shouted, putting her right leg in front of Mandy and tripping her, causing the both of them to fall.

"No!" Chloe watched them fight, instead of intervening.

"Are they seriously fighting over cups?" She asked herself. As they landed, Madison was the first to reach the door.

"Team Madison is gonna do their job first!" Madison claimed, motioning for them to follow her. Aside from her, Team Madison consisted of Chloe and Walter. Mandy and her squad followed her to the door.

"No, Team Mandy is!" Mandy retaliated. Team Mandy consisted of Mandy herself, Kendall, and Enza.

"We all know that my team will win." Brandon said. His team had him, Kelli, and Allie. The other squad, which was Ashlyn's, didn't speak because their job was to defend the ship.

"Everyone got your sky skates?" Ms. Martinez asked them all, and they all said yes, except for Madison. She jumped out of the ship.

"I don't need any skates!" She shouted, somehow learning how to fly.

"Wait, Madison! Don't leave us behind!" Chloe yelled out to her, jumping out of the ship, with Walter following her. Once she flew got above the island, she immediately slammed down on the ground due to the gravity. She tried getting up, and managed to do it.

"That was epic!" Madison shouted, and looked back at the spaceship to see Mandy laughing at her.

"You suck!" Mandy said down to her, and Madison just ran off, looking for the people that her and her team would have to fight.

"So, how many of those Epitomus people do we have to fight?" Walter asked her, catching up with her.

"2, I think." Madison answered. Chloe was flying the whole way, because of Caelum bringing out the full potential of Mythical powers.

"How are you able to even run in this gravity?" Madison asked Walter, who shrugged.

"Maybe only Sub-Legendary related to the Moon are able to, I don't know." He answered, which Madison thought it actually made sense. A blast of fire crashed down in between them, causing them to both back off.

"I found them." The Karla look alike said to the one that looked like Kandace. Madison smiled.

"Epitomus Allie is a genius at finding punching bags." She stated, watching the two land down on the ground. EP Kandace sent a wave of ice towards Madison, who jumped to dodge it. The ice caught her by the foot, so she used a burst attack with her fist to shatter it, which sent her flying upwards.

"Flaming Hell Blast!" EP Karla called out, firing off a large blast full of heat, almost at the same temperature of Mandy's, towards Madison.

"Crap!" She raised her hands to block since she had no time to counter it. Chloe teleported in front of her to deflect the blast to somewhere else.

"A tier 3 saved the tier 5. Nice."

With Team Mandy

"There they are!" Enza said, pointing towards 3 small

crystals. They were all different colors.

"Are these the Legendary Crystals?" Kendall asked, walking up to them. Mandy nodded.

"We need to take these out of her hands." Mandy responded. Kendall picked up all of them.

"Then can we fight her?"

"You know it."

BRICK OF SOUND

"ALRIGHT GUYS! LET'S GO FIND THE NEW RE-CRUITS!" Brandon shouted, using his sky skates to look around in the sky.

"Yeah!" Kelli agreed.

"Why do I have to be here?" Allie asked to no one in particular. Brandon spotted an out of place building, so he flew down to there, and they both followed.

"This is the place." Kelli said, looking inside using her goggles. Brandon got somewhat of an idea.

"How about we just pick it up?" He asked, picking up the small building with his bare hands.

"I mean, it's a good substitute if we want to get the job done fast." Allie answered.

Back with Team Madison

"Walter! Keep her in place!" Madison called out to him, reeling back a fist, which charged a large amount of Power.

"I got it!" Walter responded, using Time Control to freeze the time around EP Kandace.

"Metal Buster!" She shouted, charging towards EP Kandace with the aura around her. She then punched her in the face, which sent her flying through the clouds, and all the way down to the ground back on Earth.

"I originally made that move to deal with Alex, but if that could break steel, it does almost five times the same damage to a person." She finished, looking over to Chloe.

"I'm now the King of the Sky!" Chloe said, flying towards EP Karla. She formed a sword using the rainbow energy from her power.

"Universal Slash!" She shouted, creating a slash like attack with the sword that constantly sent EP Karla back-wards, which ended up sending her down to Earth too. Madison flew down to the island, where Walter was.

"I told you we're the best team." She said, high fiving him.

"Yeah." Mandy's team arrived at the island they were on.

"You guys were slow!" Mandy said, which got Madison somewhat mad. Madison fired off mini blasts.

"We had to fight two people! You had to steal crystals! Big difference!" She responded. Mandy pointed to the crystals that Kendall were holding.

"These crystals have the power to destroy and or save the world! You just fought two punching bags!" Madison looked at the crystals, and didn't think much of them.

"You're the punching bag." She said. A large rock had

suddenly appeared out of thin air and fell on top of her, sending her flying below the island. Since she didn't have on sky skates, she couldn't fly up there. She managed to break the rock in half, but still couldn't stop the air pressure.

"Section Leader!" She called up to her, and only Chloe could hear her. She began flying down to get her.

"I got you, bro!" Chloe shouted down to her, then catching Madison. She flew them back up onto the island.

"Thank you bro! I owe you one." Madison claimed, giving Chloe a high five.

"Don't mention it!" Brandon and his team arrived at the island. Mandy looked at him.

"Looks like you took it too literal again." Mandy said, looking at the small building in his hands. He set it down.

"You had to take crystals, and I had to rescue two people." Brandon responded, which angered Mandy.

"I told you that these crystals are very important!" She retaliated. Madison opened the door to the building while the two were arguing. Once she saw who was in there, she was surprised.

"Dad? And uncle?" Madison asked the both of them, and they were shocked too.

"Son?" One of them asked her, then the both of them came out of the building. Everyone outside were confused until they saw them.

"This is where you were Giovanna?" Mandy asked the one known as Giovanna.

"Yeah." Giovanna answered. Madison was filled with excitement.

"Dad! We all missed you!" She said.

"I missed you too son!" She responded.

"And uncle! I missed you too!"

"Did you forget what I told you to call me?" He asked her.

"No, but it looks stupid on paper." Madison answered.

"What?"

"What?" Chloe just listened to everything that was being said.

"So, Chandler is my great uncle?" She asked Madison.

"Heck yeah!" She answered. Ms. Martinez showed up on the island. She took the crystals and teleported the two using the sun energy.

"Good job guys! Meet me at the ship when your do-" Ms. Martinez began, but was soon interrupted by EP Allie showing up.

"You guys were too late." EP Allie looked down to them. Madison had been filled with fear, even though she never had that emotion in a while.

"What more do you want from us, you poor excuse for a villain!" Chloe yelled up to her. EP Allie began charging up some attack that was foreign to all of them, except for Ms. Martinez.

"Madison! Get out of here!" She shouted over to Madison, who couldn't move because of how scared she was. EP Allie used the attack on Madison, which immediately shocked her, as she was trying to take 345 away from her. She screamed in pain, as the shock was so powerful it almost completely drained her energy. EP Allie used this attack to lift her up more into the sky.

"Now I've got you!" EP Allie shouted, then laughing.

"What's she doing?" Mandy asked Ms. Martinez, who sighed.

"Full Curse Steal." Madison kept on screaming, but there was something stopping her from stealing it. The seal that was on her body was still there. The amulet that she had gotten a while ago had begun glowing.

CHAPTER 5: DAD?

"Why isn't it working?" EP Allie yelled, boosting up the shock effect, which didn't stop the amulet. The Blue Legendary crystal that was in Ms. Martinez's hands flew towards Madison and she grabbed it, which caused the attack to be negated. She dropped down to the ground, and got into a charging position.

"True hero, what'll be your next move?" EP Allie asked her, and she didn't respond. Madison charged up a lot of energy, which seemed to be coming from the crystal.

"Drive 2!" She shouted, as the energy vanished and changed into blue steam instead.

"Is Power like a car or something?" Mandy asked.

"No, there are a lot more of these. You've seen one yourself." Ms. Martinez answered. Mandy remembered what she saw.

"Negative Drive." She muttered, which Ms. Martinez nodded. Chloe herself shuddered from the energy.

BRICK OF SOUND

THE BLUE STEAM OF DRIVE 2 CALMED DOWN AFTER it was noticed that Madison had regained control Madison looked at her hands, confused with this new-found power.

"Maybe it's time for a new move set." Madison said, cracking her knuckles. EP Allie was in shock. She didn't know about the drives, or barely anything Power related, as it's so rare.

"True hero, now what's your move?" EP Allie asked Madison, who quickly teleported in front of her.

"Powerful Blaster!" She shouted, firing off a blast that was at least five times bigger than her Power Blast.

"Is this a speed form or strength?" Chloe asked Ms. Martinez.

"Drive 2 is speed focused, but also can boost strength to a degree." Ms. Martinez answered. Madison blew the smoke away from her hand.

"That's my answer." EP Allie began to become mad, which Madison didn't really care.

"I can steal everyone's powers, curses, superiority, and whatever! Why can't I steal anything from you?" She asked, which Madison just laughed at her.

"Probably cause I have something that protects me." Madison answered, only making EP Allie even more mad.

"And what's that, true hero?" Madison teleported in front of her again, only faster than last time.

"Prestige!" Madison shouted, punching her straight in the face, sending her flying. She continued laughing.

"That's payback for taking control over me." 345 Madison said through Madison's body.

"How many Madison's are there inside of that head of hers?" Mandy asked herself, which Chloe decided to answer.

"I'm pretty sure there's three, counting her." EP Allie fired off a blast of energy that was clearly not hers towards everyone else, and Madison appeared in front of them, and caught the blast. She only slid back a little bit, but she ended up completely stopping it.

"Mandy," She began.

"You scared?"

In Power World

345 Madison and another Madison, probably the one that you get from removing 345, were fighting with each other.

"I want control this time!" Power Madison shouted at the other.

"No way, I'm more needed right now." 345 Madison retaliated. Another Madison appeared, seeming to be the physical one.

CHAPTER 6: POWERFUL REACTION

"If I come back to see you guys either fighting or doing something weird again, I'm kicking the both of you out."

Back on Caelum Insula

"Why won't you die?" EP Allie asked Madison, who had returned back to the air. Madison exploded with Power again.

"Cause I want to protect my friends!" She shouted as an answer, and then the sudden burst of Power wore off.

"Her power just skyrocketed at random again. One moment she's weaker than Chloe and the next she's almost as strong as me right now." Ms. Martinez thought.

"That's a stupid reason. Maybe I'll just have to kidnap you and torture you to get the real answer out of you." EP Allie responded, which didn't affect her.

"Yeah, and? You can go ahead and try." EP Allie released a barrage of energy blasts towards Madison, which she all dodged. She motioned for her to attack her head on, which was a taunt.

"Bring it on, copycat." Mandy then crossed her arms.

"Thought that insult was made specifically for me." She said. EP Allie charged towards Madison, trying to activate a mind control attack on her, but it didn't work.

"Usually the stronger ones are easier to gain control over. That's probably what you're thinking right now." Madison claimed, dodging the charge attack she tried.

"I'm a mix between strong and weak!" EP Allie continued trying to fight her, by throwing punches, and everything she could do, but she kept on dodging. Madison pointed her hand towards her, and charged up a blast.

"I'll see you when you recover from this." Madison fired off a large blast, twice the size as Powerful Blaster, sending EP Allie all the way back down to Earthland. She dropped down to where everyone else was.

"That was epic Madison!" Chloe said to her. Madison smiled in response.

"I know, rig-" She began, but then the steam had suddenly cut off, which knocked her completely out.

"WHEN'S SHE GONNA WAKE UP?" Allie asked, sitting next to Madison, who was on the floor. Ms. Martinez crouched down and placed her hand on her face.

"I'll try putting a little energy into her." Ms. Martinez began concentrating. Madison then woke up in a cold sweat, but not on Caelum Insula. It was an endless body of water.

"Ugh, what is this place..?" The stone on her necklace separated itself from her, and began glowing.

Madison blocked the light, as it was extremely bright. Eventually, it died down, leaving a small flame like light.

"I see you've grasped onto that steam like power of yours. I can't wait to see you suffer while using it, though." Madison gave a disappointed look.

"Oh, it's you again. What do you want?" The voice

from the flame sighed.

"That trainer of yours from a while back is back in business. I'm sure you'll meet them again. By the way, your master is still gone."

"Way to remind me. Thanks for telling me that the drunk is still alive. We're definitely gonna need her help." In a quick flash, she was back on the island, slowly opening her eyes.

"Great. The idiot's back." Mandy stated, as Madison stood back up to face her.

"What'd you call me, dust pan? I'll send you 10,006 feet under." Madison countered.

"I don't want to be here anymore, bad memories. Go ahead and send me under." Mandy retaliated. Madison showed a somewhat smug expression, different from her normally neutral face.

"Really? I'd love to do that." Mandy returned with a similar look.

"Try it, you'll be going down with me." They continued arguing until they made it back to the ship.

"Alright, kid. I've got a small mission for you. A training trip!" Ms. Martinez told Madison, who was upside down on a chair.

"Cool, I guess. Does it have to do with my original trainer?" Ms. Martinez gave a confused look.

"The number one hero?""No. I must've never told you about them."

Flashback Begin

"Looks like you still have some fight in you." The trainer said, standing over Madison pridefully. After just one hit, the Power user was almost unable to move, and on the verge of passing out.

"What kind of training is it if you're just going to go all out at the start?" She complained.

"All out? Last time I went all out I accidentally destroyed a bar I was in."

"If it's you, then it's definitely not an accident. You probably did that on purpose." Madison had recovered a bit, so she stood back up.

"You can't even survive a punch from me when I'm not trying. Even if you improve after I teach you, you still wouldn't survive a minute in the Darklands."

"The what?"

Flashback End

"Oh yeah, that reminds me. The forgotten land, I remember that place! I went there once, and I almost died when I stepped foot in there!" Allie was listening in, leaning on the wall.

"I don't think you should be talking about that so lightly, Mom. Besides, once you leave, you forget everything that happened. How do you remember you went there in the first place?"

"It's not the time for conspiracy theories, Allie. I think some of my co-workers are there anyway, so it's fine for us to go after 2.0's trip." Ms. Martinez told them.

"Alright, then I'll do my best to find them! Maybe they're at my house. Haven't been there in a while." Once they landed back next to the Band House, Madison packed her bags and went on her way. Since the school wasn't so far from where she started, she thought it was a good idea to just run there as fast as she could.

Madison arrived, and the door was surprisingly unlocked. Right when she closed the door behind her, she was greeted with a punch to her face, that she blocked.

"Looks like you've improved." They said, then kicking her to the floor, not hard enough to dent it in any way.

"But not a lot." Due to it being a hardwood floor, Madison got up with her body hurting somewhat.

"Seems like you haven't improved much either, Mary." She responded, not finding any changes. Mary simply crossed her arms.

"You've got to be here for a reason. What do you want?"

"Prepare me for the Darklands." Madison boldly stated. Mary laughed, as she didn't expect this from her.

"You want me to train you for the Mysterious Forest? If you're lucky, the Gloomy Desert?" The future tenor nodded.

"It'll also help me become number one."

"You still have that dream, don't you? Well, sure, I'll train you. But, whatever time you have with me, is going to be either training, or sleeping."

"I would say thanks, but why are you in my house?" Without hesitation, Mary immediately ran away.

"That's a question that I can't answer!"

WHILE MADISON WAS OFF TRAINING, IT was up to everyone else to also train. The Darklands is a separate dimension, a more serious one, rather than the others. They had to be prepared for anything, since it's unexpected. The first place you arrive in is the Mysterious Forest, hence being unexpected. If you get lost, consider yourself gone for good.

"Try destroying this, destroyer!" Brandon sent a wave of ice using his foot in the direction of Allie, who punched and shattered the icicles in her way. Mandy was dodging sword attacks from the unexperienced Chloe. She had to get a good grip on it by the day they leave, or else they were toast.

"How do I activate Drive 2 again…?" Madison thought, trying to remember. She knew that the Power Crystal brought it out, but she doesn't know how to do it again.

"Try putting on this blindfold." Mary handed it to her, and Madison took it, then tied it around her face, covering her eyes.

"Now what?" While Madison was unable to see, Mary punched her in the face, knocking her over.

"Sorry, I just had to do that. Why don't you try powering up?" After getting up, she tried focusing on the center of her body. The steam came off, but it was extremely faint.

"It's not working. I don't feel a boost."

"Wait, I have an idea! Fight me! Don't worry, I won't go at full power." Mary ran towards Madison, who blocked every attack that came at her. The future tenor felt something touch her shoulder, so she immediately turned around to fire a blast. She couldn't tell where Mary was, which on its own is a bad thing.

"Alright, where did you go?" Madison asked.

"Find out yourself." The steam came out more and more. Mary tried to punch her again, but was blocked by Madison's foot. The aura coming off of this clash blew off the blindfold.

"Is it working?" Some of the bandages on her legs undid, which revealed heavy burn marks.

"I think so. Let's stop fighting." Madison dropped her foot, then looking down at the bandages.

"Forgot I still had these. My legs still hurt from that tournament." She fell back to sit down, the steam disappearing.

"Or is it from that time when I s-"

"Nope. Definitely not. Anyway, what do you think activated Drive 2?"

"It's probably fear. You know that you won't die from something like that, but you're still scared. So, your body kicks into overdrive."

"Didn't know I had any emotions, but I guess that's fine for something bad. Come on, teach me how to make Drive 2 last!" Meanwhile, at the training spot, Ms. Martinez was giving Mandy her final lesson.

"So, has your power been giving you any troubles?" The hero asked the future oboe, who shook her head.

"Not really. Aside from feeling weaker sometimes, it's been perfectly fine." Ms. Martinez pondered this for a moment.

"Maybe training harder would help? You need to practice going below full strength, mainly for stealth reasons, but partly so you don't accidentally cause trouble." Ms. Martinez was very good at pointing out flaws.

"Okay. As long as I can beat that idiot," Mandy began, looking at Brandon. As if he had a sixth sense for this, he looked over to her.

"What was that? Are you picking a fight with me?"

"I don't mind training." She finished, then walking over to the Bari. Brandon began cracking his knuckles.

"Don't cry when I beat you to the ground, 'Stupid Tenor!'" He exclaimed.

"I'd say the same thing, 'Oversized Alto!'" Mandy instantly shot flames at him, which was blocked by his ice. He only had it for a few days, and he already had a good handle on it.

"Should we stop them?" Allie asked Walter, who she was training with.

"Nah, let them be. We can't really do anything with these things." He responded, showing her the heavy bracelets they had on.

"I forgot about these. I wish we could take the limiters off, they're really restricting." Allie stated, gaining a disappointed look from the trumpet.

"That's why they're called limiters, Allie."

"Oh. Wait a minute, James has been on that mission for a longer time than usual."

"Good point, we can go find him now." They began

walking off, but they were stopped by Ms. Martinez.

"Even though you two are part of our strongest, you still aren't strong enough to go the Darklands yet. Maybe you should get b-" She was interrupted by Allie.

"But Mom, we are better! We've been better! You just won't let us go at full power!" She yelled, making Walter back off, not wanting to be involved.

"That's because I don't want you to get hurt. Maybe you can take the limiters off next time."

"It's always next time! You said that when I went through the Band Festival! Why won't you just let us go full throttle?" While angry, the energy from her unknown attack would radiate off of her.

"Because you're supposed to be kids, not pro heroes! You're supposed to enjoy the challenge of the limits! Maybe you'll realize when you're older!" Ms. Martinez countered. Unable to respond, Allie stormed off, probably not coming back for a while. For defense training, Alex had the rest of the Kelli Squad, plus Ashlyn, train by attacking him all at once. For stamina training, Chloe kept the sword out for long periods of time while alternating between fighting Brandon, Mandy, and Amy.

"What day is it…?" Madison mumbled, waking up. "The day you're supposed to go back." Mary told her.

"Ah, okay. Wait, why are you in my bed?" The aspiring hero shot out of the room, hiding behind the door frame.

"I thought you'd be lonely by yourself, since you're so used to that."

"Whatever! Go pack my bags, I have to be there soon." Madison walked away, just to sit down in front of the front door. Her week of training was mostly uneventful, aside from just being drained from training all day. Even though she just woke up, she was struggling to keep herself awake, due to being so tired. With all that aside, she still improved a lot.

"Here!" Mary threw a bag towards Madison, which she caught with one finger. She then opened the door.

H, A CHAPTER FOCUSING ON THE OTHER SIDE? Characters that we haven't met before? Here you go.

"A normal day in the Darklands?" Kim asked, in denial of the day not having anything weird.

"Yeah, surprisingly. Maybe we'll find a foreigner or two on our grounds." Bailey answered. The lower and bass clarinets were a part of the royal guard. Sure, they were clarinets, but not of royalty like the first clarinets. It seemed like the clarinets were used like weapons.

"It's really weird how you didn't get banished, you know, for that accusation with the kn-"

"You aren't banished even though you're a creep!" Some clarinets were banished from the land, and ended up with Ms. Martinez. But, they had to keep some of the royal guard, as a fighting force to protect the royal family. Did they know who were a part of that family, not necessarily. They only knew it was the better clarinets than they, though the bass clarinets are just grouped with the lower.

"Fancy clothes for kids." A voice said, alerting Bailey to point her bass clarinet towards the two figures.

"Out of all of Darklands, you guys should know what royal outfits look like."

"We're foreigners, from Earthland. I would assume your king has told you about us." The other voice told the two, making Bailey drop her defenses.

"Did he?" She asked Kim, who shrugged.

"I don't pay attention during meetings."

"Oh yeah. I forgot you're useless. Carry on with your day!" The two guards walked away, leaving the tourists there.

"That was oddly easy." When the two were outside of the Negative Kingdom, they heard a small noise gradually get louder, getting closer. It was a rather small motorcycle with about 5 people on it. Did the Darklands have automobiles? No.

"Hey, it's you guys! How've you been?" The one with goggles questioned, getting the one driving to stop so she could get off to greet them.

"Kelli? What're you doing here? You know it's against the law, right?" Kim responded.

"Well, that's too bad. The Kelli Squad goes where they want!" Another one said, also approaching them.

"What a stupid name." Bailey laughed.

"I know, it sucks." A voice they knew agreed.

"Aaliyah! You're here too?" Kim attempted throwing her clarinet at her, but Aaliyah made it float.

"Against my will, yes."

"Aside from that weird object you guys are using as transportation; we definitely could sneak you in." Bailey brought up.

"That makes our job a lot easier. I'll go tell Ms. Martinez about this." The driver stated, then going on their way.

"Come on, introduce us to your friends! You know how it is here, we can't have those!" Kim begged Aaliyah.

"This is Kandi." She told them.

"Yes, this indeed is Kandi. What's good?" Kandi patted Kim on the shoulder.

"What weird language you use." Bailey laughed yet again.

"That's a lot of complaining from someone who can't use power in the kingdom." Aaliyah responded.

"Again, those were allegations! Not real!"

"Then who were the two that went away?" Kim questioned.

"That's Walter and Enza. They'll introduce themselves properly when you guys visit our base." Kelli explained

"Dang, you already built an entire base here? You guys are definitely rebelling against the king."

A few hours later

Using technology from Walter, they had their entire base stored in a small capsule like object. The base was small, compared to the Band House. It wasn't that different in layout, since they each got their own room. In the center of the house, it was just a table covered in mission plans.

"Now that we've got some guard royal people, let's interrogate you two." Kandi tried to do, before interrupted by Enza.

"There's no need for interrogation. More of..." She pointed the still floating clarinet towards Kim.

"...intenorgation." The only people who found the joke funny were Kim and Kandi, the others either not focused or not interested.

"Jokes aside, we still need to learn about this place.

Who runs this place?" Walter asked the two.

"You see, we can't tell you. We can tell you that he's our king, but we can't give any other info. Since we're technically off duty, I can tell you a little secret." Bailey explained.

"Wait, no! We swore not to tell anyone about that, especially foreigners!" Kim exclaimed.

"It's fine to break rules every now and then. So, listen for this one time only. The king isn't really in charge."

"What does that mean?" Kandi asked.

"Our kingdom is overrun by cursed instruments. All of the people who were killed in the Civil War that we had haunted the instruments."

"And what does this have to do with the king?" Kelli questioned.

"It's because the amount of energy that the instruments release began corrupting our king, and soon enough, the whole Negative Kingdom!" Kim attempted to scare them, only succeeding with Kandi.

"So you guys aren't affected by this energy?" Walter asked, as the two both shook their heads.

"The more powerful, the easier it is to be corrupted. The king is very strong, way stronger than all of us combined, and times like, a thousand!" Kim tried scaring them again, still with the same outcome.

"That's an exaggeration. But, as proper introductions, I'm Bailey, captain of the bass clarinet corps."

"I'm Kim, the lieutenant of the clarinet corps. For extra information, Bailey has a court case to go to for stealing a bass clari-"

"Stop telling people that!" Kelli finished her mission report and taped it to the wall.

"Someone's missing." She sensed. Kandi counted everyone there.

"I think we're fine." After she spoke, an explosion was

heard further throughout the Mysterious Forest. When they arrived to find the cause, all they found was Madison against a tree, almost lifeless.

"The instruments got to her." Bailey stated, getting Aaliyah to pick her up.

"Come on, let's take Madison to the ship." Walter told them, as they began walking away.

BRICK OF SOUND

WAT ELSE IS IN DARKLANDS, ASIDE FROM bored guards just wandering around? Well, there's the mystery people from earlier! But who were they? Guess we'll find out soon.

"Instruments are stronger here, right?" Amy asked, holding her flute as if it were a sword. She had Kendall make a sheath for it, so she could use it to fight, and also put it away safely without taking it apart.

"Yeah, by a lot. It really depends on the person. Someone like Kim wouldn't be able to make a scratch on the ground." Bailey answered.

"That's actually hard to do in the forest. Those trees are like steel!" Amy immediately went outside to look at the trees.

"Watch this, Alex!" He was on watch duty, making sure that no one did anything suspicious. When she gained his attention, she sliced through a tree like it was butter, then sheathing the flute.

"What was that for?"

"Nothing." Due to the answer being vague to him, Amy left him confused outside, walking back inside.

"At least you can just carry the thing around like it's nothing." Allie told her. Amy took the instrument out and tried weighing it.

"The flute feels way lighter than normal. It's like I'm holding a stick."

"Really?" Brandon asked excitedly, then getting the Bari out to hold. He lifted it with one finger, despite that not being exactly safe.

"Yeah, it feels like nothing! No clue how I'd hit people with it, though." He wanted to test it out badly, but his main challenger was busy waking up Madison.

In Power World

"So, you're fusing into me?" Madison asked the now combined 345 and Power, along with Superiority.

"We decided that it was the only way to save you. I'll increase your base stats, 345 will keep you alive longer, and Power will just make you more experienced." Superiority Madison explained.

"Wait, you can't just leave! You're gonna make me more unstable! I can't handle three people at a time!"

"That's not how it works. You'll get a lot of buffs, the only debuff is that this world will vanish."

"...you do realize if you guys disappear now, I won't remember your existence. I'll remember the powers, but not the memories." The two began vanishing, making Power World crumble in pieces.

"Can't you handle yourself?" They stated at the same

time, and begun glowing. The future tenor just stared at the light.

"No, I-"

In the Darklands

"The disable isn't working. That's suspicious." Mandy thought, narrowing her eyes while looking at Madison's Power Seal.

"Can't!" Madison shouted, waking up unexpectedly. She almost hit Mandy in the face, but missed and hit her forehead.

"Ow! What's your deal?" The future oboe questioned Madison, who was hurt as well.

"I don't know, what's yours?" They went back and forth until an instrument case was thrown at the Power user. Madison identified it as the tenor that Mandy had used.

"I know you're still recovering, but use this to fight." After mentioning recovering, Madison realized that due to fusing with 345, her recovery speed had increased. Even with the bandages, she still felt better than ever. Must have been a Prestige boost.

"You think I'm weak? Get ready for this!" She gripped the handle tight, along with Mandy, and bolted out of her room to the forest. Madison seemed more agile, as she was jumping through trees.

"Woah! Slow down for once!" Madison laughed.

"For once?" Spotting a person, she stopped and landed on the ground floor in front of them.

"You're not from here, are you?" Mandy stepped forward, putting her hand in front of Madison, to stop her from intervening.

"Nope. We come from Earthland." She ran at them

and attempted blasting them, but they dodged, and tapped her. She was about to counter, but was met with her own blast.

"Blaze, right? That's a Sub-Legendary, yeah?" The person asked Mandy, who was confused.

"That's a weird power! I've got to write that down." Madison stated, still holding the tenor. A figure appeared behind her and took out an alto to attack, but was blocked with her case.

"No wonder you're having issues, captain." They said sarcastically, striking multiple times while Madison used the case as a shield.

"Quit it, William. You're just salty that you can't become captain."

"Jeez, I'm sorry, Sidney. You know the king is rigging the results." They both backed off from the two on the defensive.

"You guys should help us on our trip. We're looking for three people." Madison brought up.

"Okay, sure. As long as there's food." William responded, as the two rivals dropped their guard.

"I'm pretty sure the ship is that way, so follow us!" Mandy hopped on Madison's back and they zoomed off, with the new recruits not that far behind from them too.

"Guess we got some altos. Probably not for long." Madison said, running around the trees in her path.

"Not like we want any, but it's nice to have more firepower." While the tenors were retrieving the new allies, Brandon went on a small trip to get a chance to look around. Because of his power, which leads into destruction, he's never usually allowed away from Ms. Martinez's watch. It was special circumstances though, so he'll be fine. Right?

"Weight Binding." A voice said, making Brandon's arms stick together, combined with heavy weights, which was around one ton.

"You Epitomus people, always sneaking up on future pros. What do you want?" He asked, not able to find where the person was. He was transferred to an underground base.

"I have a request to ask of you." EP Allie told the Bari, who still stood strong in front of her, not intimidated.

BRICK OF SOUND

"H MM...SO THEY'RE IN THE CITY." Ms. Martinez pondered, walking in multiple directions, ultimately reaching a dead end which was a tree. A large tree, at that.

"Is this the city?" She thought it looked a tad bit suspicious, but she was unable to comprehend that it definitely wasn't a city. At lightning speed, a figure attempted to land a kick on Ms. Martinez, who blocked it.

"You still have your guard up, even since a few years back." Ms. Martinez coughed, as steam came out. Perhaps from over exhaustion? It seemed that she blocked it with not much difficulty, though.

"I've got a lot to tell you, Señora. Especially with my condition." After a small amount of time, they went into the tree, which had an invisible barrier. It worked as a very disguised base, despite its size difference from the rest of the trees. Sitting in a chair, Ms. Martinez explained everything from the events of the Band Festival to that of Caelum Insula.

"That's an interesting situation. You need to take a break eventually, or else you'll die." Señora Salcedo understood, and she was right. In the basics, her limits were overcome in Epitomus, and her power was diminishing. Gradually, not that fast. If she goes over her limits again, she won't have that much time left.

"Come on, it's not that bad. I'm still strong enough. By the way, where's Stevens?" Ms. Martinez asked.

"I sent her to your spaceship to find you, but here you are. She'll show up eventually." In the underground base, Brandon was waiting for EP Allie to ask the question.

"Do you want to join me on a path to power? To get stronger than the rest of your friends?" She questioned. Brandon began laughing.

"Me? Join a low life villain like you? No chance in hell! As long as she's alive, I won't drift in the slightest!" He mocked, his aura alone slowly cracking the weights. The superiority glow sent chills through EP Allie.

"So you don't want to get stronger? Not even stronger than this she you mention?" EP Allie continued questioning him.

"Of course I do! Not with a weakling on my side! The only thing you can do is control, not contain!" He broke through the weights and used a rocket to blast through the base walls and the ground, and arose from grass, still in the forest.

"Always underestimating Baris, like always. Whatever. I'll just make my own impact on the world." He put his hands in his pockets and went on his way through the forest.

CHAPTER 11: LIMITATION

In the Spaceship

Everything is relatively the same without Ms. Martinez. Except, the spaceship has somehow ended up in the desert. The seemingly endless desert.

"Don't worry guys, I'll find us a way out of this!" Madison claimed, removing Allie from the pilot seat just to start pressing random buttons.

"Hey! Get out of the chair! You don't know what you're doing!" Allie exclaimed, kicking Madison into the door that lead to the center, breaking it entirely.

"It's safe to say none of us do. If only Brandon was here to lift us up or something." Chloe brought up, as he was indeed missing. A figure turned the spaceship weightless from outside, and began carrying it. They ran fast, not too long after arriving in front of the tree base, putting it down.

"That was some work." They said, then going into the base. Everyone in the spaceship was left confused.

"Uh...what?" Madison asked, now floating upside down. She was the only one affected by the gravity change, despite it being over. The figure dusted off their hands.

"Your kids are a lot of work, Martinez." They told Ms. Martinez, who nodded.

"Yeah, they are. Wait a minute, you're back!" She shouted. They gave her a thumbs up.

"Stevens, reporting for duty! I've retrieved the target!" Ms. Stevens told the two. Ms. Martinez became excited.

"Perfect timing! I have to introduce you to the kids." She said.

"This person right here is the number three hero, Luna!" Ms. Martinez introduced her, she and Madison saying the hero name at the same time.

"Yeah, I know you! You took care of me once when Ms. Martinez had hero work!" Madison remembered.

"So, the number one hero has the power of the sun, and you have the power of the moon?" Mandy questioned her.

"Yup! Legendary moon power, in the flesh!" Ms. Stevens proudly answered.

"Very inconsistent when it comes to power hierarchy." Chloe said.

"Power hierarchy has nothing to do with hero ranking. It's based off a point system. I only became number one because of my super awesome rise in popularity!" Ms. Martinez responded.

"Explains how weak you are."

"What?!"

"So, tell me, what was it, Kim? Pretty sure. But, tell me about your ruler." Enza questioned the clarinet guard.

"Before the instruments came in, he wasn't really that far off from Ms. Martinez. I mean, since we're in separate dimensions, powers are respawned here. You can meet people in the Darklands who have the same power as you." She explained, then picking up her clarinet.

"Then what's yours?" Kim sighed.

"To be honest, I haven't told anyone this yet, but I really don't have one. The spinner with thousands of powers gave me nothing."

"Don't worry about it! Being powerless doesn't matter, what matters is your ambition! What's your dream?" Enza asked.

"Uh…" Kim began.

"I don't know. The only thing we can do is protect Darklands and the king. What about yours?"

"To be the number one hero, against the wishes of where I'm from! Going into some detail, we also have royal families in Earthland. I was destined to rise to the throne, but long story short, I ended up where I am now, in peace with Walter and the rest of the Kelli Squad."

"We all have our dreams. Once you find out yours, we'll be grateful to accept you into the band." Ms. Martinez appeared out of nowhere, only scaring Kim since the ones already in the band were used to it.

"Okay, I guess I'll think about it." While they were talking, Madison began practicing her attacks against Brandon.

"Get ready for this, Impact Man!" She joked, meeting his kick with hers.

"It's 'The Impact'! Get it right!" Brandon transferred ice from his leg to try to freeze her, but right when it touched her foot, Madison blasted herself away. She brought her hand up to her face, covering it in 345 markings.

"Alright then, my hero name is…" She trailed off, trying to think of a name mid battle.

"The enemy wouldn't stop for you!" He slammed his fist into her hand, which she caught and flipped him over.

"On your feet and fight me like a Bari!" Chloe charged in, attempting to hit Brandon with a blast, who dodged it by flipping himself backwards.

"Come on and face me then!" The two clashed, sparks of lightning come off their punches. Madison simply walked off, not having anything to do anymore. She eventually made it to the Kelli Squad Hideout, where Ms. Martinez was. Madison walked in.

"Hey kids, any interesting going on?" She asked, as Kelli lifted her goggles.

"Actually, yeah! There's a tournament being held by the king, and we can fight in it since no one wants to participate." Kelli answered, gaining a nod from the future tenor.

"That's cool, but why don't they want to join? A tournament every once in a while, and they obviously need a break." Kim decided to respond.

"It's cause the king fights the winner! Everyone dies in the end!" Ms. Martinez thought about that.

"I'd like to see him try killing me. I'm gonna join the tournament!" She claimed.

"Fine, that means I'll join, Ms. Martinez! I'll show you how fabulous my Drive 2 is!" She tried to imitate how Ms. Martinez moves around when fighting, but ended up on the ground.

"So, when's the tourney?" Walter asked Kim, who placed a huge poster on the wall.

"The Day of the Ceremony!" No one knew what it was, until Bailey decided to speak up.

"It's tomorrow." She stated, surprising everyone in the room.

"Wait, give me a sec." Madison got out her phone, and began calling someone. The person in question picked up.

"What do you want me to make?" Kendall asked, working on some robot.

"Ah, nothing! Just tell everyone there that there's a tournament tomorrow."

"Okay." Madison hung up. She got in a fighting pose.

"You're permanently at 50%, so let's see how strong I am against it. Remember, it's practice!" She told Walter, who simply pointed one arm in Madison's direction.

"I'll take that challenge!" Knowing his tactics, before he could put her in a time lock, Madison dodged to the right. Madison didn't want to destroy the Kelli Squad Base, so she ran outside. Walter appeared behind her, and thanks to Mary's training, was blasted in the face by Madison, who backed up.

"If only you could get those weights off." Madison told him, crossing her arms. He looked at them.

"Yeah, they're the worst." They continued to battle, until Madison thought it was a good idea to leave, so she went back to the spaceship.

"Hey, ga-" Before she could finish, she was kicked in the face by both Brandon and Chloe, who were still fighting.

"Section Leader! What're you doing here?" Chloe exclaimed, holding onto the now smoking tenor.

"I don't remember…" Madison mumbled as an answer, then passing out.

"Look what you did, you killed her!" Brandon shouted.

"That was your fault!" Chloe retaliated.

THE DARKLANDS TOURNEY HAD STARTED, BEING watched by the royal family. Amy got in a fight with one of the guards and took their outfit prior. It was completely unnecessary, but she did it any-way. Her fight was against Kelli.

"Alright, you ready?" The clarinet asked the flute, who simply unsheathed her flute.

"To beat you again, of course." Once the king gave the signal to fight, Kelli immediately flew into the air.

"Some wins are won by ringouts!" She blasted Amy with water, which was swiftly cut through by the flute.

"I'm not an idiot." Amy stated, jumping up into the air, right in front of the leader.

"Flute Style: Middle C Drop Fling!" She teleported behind her, and they both landed on the ground. Amy put her flute back in the sheath, activating the rest of the attack. Kelli flew backwards, out of the ring, and onto the floor.

"That was way faster than last time." Madison remembered, thinking about the last fight.

"That's what sh-" Kim began, before being blasted in the face by the former. Mandy's fight was next, as she was going against Kendall.

"I heard you're gonna be a double reed like me. It's about time to see if you deserve the title!" She released a few small blasts from her right hand.

"Yeah, I do! I'm going to be the bassoon!" When the signal was given, Kendall turned his arm into the phoenix form to block multiple oncoming blasts from the current tenor.

"Oh! You want to block?" She taunted, using a flame to maneuver around him. She almost struck, but was punched back by his normal hand.

"I don't really have good fighting techniques, so yeah! I'll defend for as long as I want to!"

"Really? That won't matter in the end." Mandy stated, charging a compressed energy blast. Kendall turned into his full phoenix form, flying up into the air. She shot the blast, only for it to be kicked away. Using that as a distraction, Mandy used a sledgehammer like attack to knock him down into the arena, leaving a small crater. After 10 seconds passed, he was still out for the count, meaning Mandy won. Once Kendall was taken out, the next battle was prepared.

"These are some fast battles. We need a longer fight." Madison commentated, as Brandon got his match against Aaliyah.

"You bass clarinets have no chance against me!" He beckoned, covering his hands in ice. When the match started, her gravity effect activated, lifting him on the ground. He stacked more ice on his arm, until he was completely grounded.

"Even if he's an idiot, he's still a great tactician." Mandy brought up, appearing right next to Madison, who wasn't shocked in the slightest.

"You aren't wrong. Maybe he'd be great in some sort of war." To scare Aaliyah into forfeiting, he transferred the ice to the ground, and it began rushing towards her. It stopped right in her face, so she backed up. Right when she did, the ice surrounded Aaliyah, making the Bari smirk.

"I've got you cornered. What're you gonna do now?"

"Not be a try-hard like you." The smirk turned into an angrier expression.

"What?!" Brandon exclaimed, then flying up into the air. He lost control of the ice, so it melted.

"I forgot how bad the flaws my best students had were." Ms. Martinez facepalmed.

"They can't be that bad." Ms. Stevens responded.

"Well, Brandon is easily distracted by insults, Mandy is easily persuaded, Chloe still has a villain side, and don't even get me started with Big 3." She explained.

"It's not that bad. At least they have some inspiration, since out of all of the choices, you became number one."

"Come on, you don't even have to go that far!" Brandon quickly adapted to being in the air, using rockets at his feet to fly down. He used the arena as some sort of spring, then changed his direction over to Aaliyah, who fell out of the ring before they could collide. Since she touched the floor first, it was fine for Brandon to land on the ground.

"My point stands. But still, it's weird how you haven't been noticed by the king." Brandon whispered, only being heard by the Mythical power users. He helped her up, only to effortlessly toss her into the stands, with him following. Madison stepped on the rails.

"Get ready for this Kim!" She jumped off onto the arena, landing in what she would call an epic pose. Alex got onto the stage as well.

"That was trash!" Allie shouted to Madison, who responded by using a small bit from superiority glow to intimidate her, which ultimately was useless.

"Eh, whatever. Anyway, it's time we fought again. When was our last fight? Like, 2 months ago?" Madison attempted at making a conversation.

"Yeah, it was. This time, I'm going to win." Alex said, as all it did was get Madison to laugh.

"That was a funny joke." Right when the signal was given, she instantly tapped into Drive 2 to appear in front of him. As if she had seen into the future, when he turned his arm into metal, Madison teleported behind him and kicked him in the back, regretting it right after. She looked down at her legs.

"I have to be careful going against him, since I have to use these less. My body can only handle moving with these, not attacking." She went on a long thought process before snapping back into the fact that Alex almost punched her in the face, and she dodged on instinct.

"You're definitely faster." He covered both of his arms in platinum and released a barrage of punches towards the tenor. All of them were countered with blasts. Eventually, he stopped attacking.

"It's critic time! You can now use two platinum arms, meaning you've gotten better at that. Everything else improved from you, except for stamina. Maybe you should work on that weakness!" She told him, placing a fist on one hand. Madison fired Horizontal Slash, which he dodged, by moving to the right.

"I don't take criticism from a fake saxophone." Alex responded, trying to strike Madison with his flute, but he was blocked by the tenor case. Even when it was in horrible shape, it proved to be a sturdy shield in the Darklands.

"Suit yourself." Madison thought of a good idea.

If she could trick him into wasting all of his energy in one punch, she could win. Enacting this idea, she taunted Alex by motioning for him to fight her.

"Such a chicken for the future number one. Maybe I should just take your spot!" She began, getting Alex to clench his fist.

"Not a chance." He wanted to charge after her, but he had a gut feeling that it was a trap.

"You only want to be number one to put plant life back on Earth! You should've stayed in Epitomus!" Madison finished, which set Alex off. He jumped into the air, put his arms into an X formation, and turned them into platinum.

"You don't tell me what to do!" Alex shouted, getting closer and closer to Madison. Right before he could land the deciding blow, Madison gripped his arms as hard as she could, and threw him at the wall behind her. Alex hit the wall, then fell down to the ground.

"Ow, ow! I might've broken something." Madison mumbled, as she put her hands to their limits, maybe even above that. She then jumped back to her seat.

"This is a pretty nice tournament, seeing that you're participating." Señora Salcedo added, watching Ms. Martinez step onto the half-destroyed arena. She put her fists together.

"Of course it is! I mean, it's fun to challenge my students to see how good they are!" She said excitedly.

"You're just doing that because you want a fight." Ms. Stevens countered.

"Well, I haven't exactly fought in a tournament in like, what, a decade? That was my pro hero exams." She responded.

"That made me seem very old, thank you." Señora Salcedo stated, getting ready to watch the second to last final fight for the preliminaries.

"Is this tournament to your liking?" The presumably Darklands King asked a figure next to them, who had on an outfit similar to the Royal Guard, this time equipped with a cape.

"Yes, it is." Allie was about to jump from the railing, but she overheard this conversation from some unknown reason. She turned to Walter.

"You heard that too?" Allie asked the trumpet, who nodded.

"Yeah, it's definitely got to be him."

DUE TO HER MATCH BEING A WHILE AWAY, Madison decided to go on a quick detour alone. It was risky for a power user of such a high caliber to go by themselves, but she didn't really care. Her first spot was a base hidden under moss, while the inside was completely renovated, including a table for three.

"Intruder alert!" Madison stated, breaking down the entrance. Right when she did, she was almost punched by a figure, but she ducked and moved out of the way to face them.

"Welcome to the Darklands." A figure said behind the other. The first figure was golden, and was surrounded by floating ZBoxes.

"Gary! What're you doing here?" Madison asked, as Gary returned the figure back to him. He pointed at Madison.

"No, what're you doing in the Darklands? Aren't you

from Earthland?" He questioned back, making the tenor point back.

"Yes, I am, but that's besides the point! How does the Internet spread so fast through the two dimensions?"

"No clue. Where's Ruby and Mr. No Tengo?" She asked, and Gary shrugged.

"I sent them to the town to go buy some juice. I also need a new TV, cause I broke it with Project Gotham cause it wouldn't stop playing these stupid commercials." He explained, gaining a nod from the tenor.

"That's why you were angry that day. Alright, makes sense. See you later, weeb." Madison walked over the doors she broke and made her way to another base. Even though the two were far apart she still found her way there.

What was going on while she was gone? The tournament, of course! Allie was now fighting against Ms. Martinez. While constantly trading blows, the two were having a conversation.

"So, how's that anger of yours doing?" Ms. Martinez asked, as Allie blocked her kick.

"It's the same, obviously. Are you asking about the limiters?" Ms. Martinez dodged her counterpunch.

"Yes, I have to make sure you don't have your blood boiling during an organized match. Remember what happened last time?" Allie deflected her blast out of the way, which had a trail of smoke.

"I still got my hero license, didn't I?" They both moved back a bit.

"Perfect score, too. But that doesn't make you any better than the other Big 3, since they got the same score." Ms. Martinez stated. Allie shrugged.

"Still." Madison was jumping through trees, then tripped over a branch. Once she fell, she screamed while falling into a building, crashing down onto the floor.

"Madison! What're you doing here?" A person exclaimed, throwing a flame at her. Madison moved out of the way, and it went flying out of the door.

"Ah, it's you! That person from my 4th block!" She responded, as they emerged from the shadows.

"The name's Melissa, the banished warrior!"

"You're not really a warrior, all you did was get sent here on accident." Madison deadpanned.

"Cut the crap and leave!" Melissa picked up the tenor, and threw her over the forest at high speeds. Madison landed right in front of the arena.

"Scary…" She walked back into her seat. Right when she sat down, Kim smacked her across the face. Madison countered by punching her in her arm, doing more damage than what the former did.

"So, what's been going on in the battle?" Madison asked Kim, who held her clarinet tightly.

"That Ms. Martinez person…" She began.

"…is amazing, right?" The royal guard nodded.

"I know exactly what you're feeling right now. It's like her presence gives off this aura of heat, but it's not as strong as it used to be. Training with her was hard, even during winter months!" Madison explained.

"Just a heads up, before you fight the king, you have to travel to his palace. It's across the desert. Just like with our tradition, when the tournament ends, it's back to dark skies." Bailey told her from behind her.

"So it's not normally this bright?" Chloe questioned Bailey, who shook her head.

"Nah. Recently, it's been dying out. As we said, when the tournament ends, it goes pitch black, and gets brighter." Kim said to Madison.

"Okay, so do we have to switch clothes for this reason?" Mandy questioned the two.

"Your clothes have to be all black, or else the sun will burn you!" Kim attempted to scare them, but as normal, only scared Kandi.

"I guess that makes sense." They went back to watching the fight, which ultimately had gone nowhere. Blast after blast, counter after counter, it seemed like they were equal. Like they knew each other's fighting Madison.

"You're not going at full power, mom." Allie said to Ms. Martinez.

"I actually have a reason for that. You know why, we live together." Kim looked at

"Your presence is nothing like any of the rest of them. Like, artificial or something like that." Bailey agreed.

"You're right for the first time. You see, us royal guard are trained to be able to perceive the difference between bad and good. The king, for example, used to have good, but is slowly going bad." Madison thought a little.

"Then again, I don't have any clue what I'm aligned with. Some heroes turn out to be bad, and some villains turn out to be good, like Section Leader."

"I knew something was wrong with your aura." Bailey said to Chloe, who forced a grin.

"No clue what you're talking about." Due to Ms. Martinez's power diminishing slowly, she decided to end the fight quickly.

"Hey, Allie! If you can land this last hit on me, I'll give you your pro license!" The number one hero shouted over to the other side of the arena. Allie was immediately intrigued.

"Really? Alright!" She prepared a bit, then dashed towards Ms. Martinez. She got so close to punching her, but as if she could see the future, the hero dodged. Allie turned around to land another strike. Ms. Martinez kicked her out of the ring before she could.

CHAPTER 14: STROLL AWAY

"Guess you'll have to do it the old-fashioned way now." They returned to their seats, and it was time for the final round of the preliminaries. Right when the match started, though…

"I forfeit." Walter stated bluntly.

"Uh… Alright." Chloe said.

"Surprisingly easy." Madison laughed.

BRICK OF SOUND

Chapter 15
A STRANGE MISHAP

IN CASE YOU HAVEN'T NOTICED, THE TOURNAMENT bracket, is rather, odd. It seems as whoever wins in the actual finals has to fight Ms. Martinez. Whoever wins in that standoff has to fight the King.

"Alright, get ready for this!" Mandy shouted. She was fighting against Amy this round.

"I can't wait to see you lose!" Amy responded.

"Rock...Paper..." They both began.

"Scissors!" Mandy took out paper, and Amy took out rock.

"Are you serious? I shouldn't have agreed to a game with a duck!" Albeit reluctantly, she went to her seat. Mandy also did so. Now, it's time for the final whatever round between Madison and Brandon.

"We're one of the same, you know? Curse, power, and superiority!" Madison brought up. Once realizing, the Bari laughed a small bit.

"You aren't wrong. Let's see if you can keep up with me!" The signal was given, and Brandon immediately rocketed into the air. Madison turned on Drive 2, jumping as high as he was. As ice barely grazed her, the tenor punched him in the face. Some ice had gotten on her fist.

"Looks like I can! Tenor Turbo!" Madison grabbed his face, despite more ice spreading on her body, and used Power to blast herself at very high speeds down into the arena. She almost destroyed it in the process.

"Very resourceful, but at a cost." Allie narrated, as the smoke cleared. Brandon had made armor out of his ice, it having spikes across his body. Madison's right arm was completely covered, and she was somewhat exhausted. The steam was getting stronger at the moment.

"Don't you know I'm practically invincible now? The ice is way stronger than my power." Brandon explained. He was right. True Strength is the perfect offense, and the Frost Curse was the perfect defense. This was going to be a tough fight for our Power user.

...or was it?

"Burst!" Madison called out, using her finger to in turn break the ice on her arm, and also the spike parts of his armor.

"That all you can do without breaking your arms?" Brandon taunted. 345 began appearing, with the lines reaching her face.

"Nope. Sure, you may be impenetrable, but you're just an ice cube!" Using child logic, she used the dark energy of 345 to melt his ice. It wasn't gradually. Not even close. It went straight through it, then disappearing. She sighed, as 345 vanished.

"You want to continue, or end it here?" Brandon attempted to run towards her, but he ran out of energy fast.

"I'm not going to lose here!" He exclaimed.

CHAPTER 15: A STRANGE MISHAP

"The curse energy fused with your energy. You used up all of your ice as a shield on yourself, meaning when it was destroyed, so was your energy." Madison told him. It was information new to the both of them. 345 told her that not too long before it fused with her.

"...fine. I forfeit." He said, just going into the arena instead of his seat. A break was started so they could recover before the finals (technically). Madison went to one of the waiting rooms to hopefully fall asleep.

"You're not Mandy. She wouldn't lose a chance to fight someone strong just for a rock paper scissors match!" Brandon told Mandy, whose eyes changed color.

"Caught me red handed, didn't you? Well, she agreed to this!" It was EP Allie's voice coming out of her body. Knowing that it was still Mandy, he punched her clean across the face, as his energy was slowly coming back.

"I knew we couldn't trust that faker. She probably did it for a reason." Brandon thought. EP Allie came back to her senses.

"You wouldn't hurt your dear friend, would you?" EP Allie asked. Without hesitation, Brandon picked her up by her collar, slowly freezing it.

"She ain't my friend, more of an annoyance! She isn't a scaredy cat like you!" In fear, EP Allie left Mandy's body, returning her to her normal state.

"Let go of me, snowman!" Mandy kicked him in the stomach, knocking both of them away from each other.

"What's with you, traitor?" The Bari asked angrily.

"You need to know something about my family." Mandy told him, which put the emotions he was showing back inside him. On the other side, Madison was now upside down in a chair.

"People with their spirit chains connected to another person's." Madison thought out loud. If you're able to see spirit chains, you could note that every person has theirs connected to another. Well, Madison's chains are wrapped around herself, and there's multiple locks around it.

"Not fair." She mumbled. Ms. Martinez walked in, which made Madison flip herself up.

"Remember, if you win, I won't go easy on you!" She told the future tenor, who nodded in excitement.

"Of course! I won't go easy either!" She wasn't just excited for a possible battle against her favorite hero. She was also excited for the adventure that entails after! Through a desert through darkness so dark it'll burn you if you don't have black on. Since she mainly wore black all the time (including her hero outfit), it was practically calling for her.

"Not fair." She mumbled. Ms. Martinez walked in, which made Madison flip herself up.

"Remember, if you win, I won't go easy on you!" She told the future tenor, who nodded in excitement.

"Of course! I won't go easy either!" She wasn't just excited for a possible battle against her favorite hero. She was also excited for the adventure that entails after! Through a desert through darkness so dark it'll burn you if you don't have black on. Since she mainly wore black all the time (including her hero outfit), it was practically calling for her.

"Well, of course, if I went full power like I did in Epitomus, I'd definitely win!" Right after Ms. Martinez said that, steam would rush out of her in a burst, making her kneel. It did go away, but it left her particularly drained. Madison went over to help her up.

"I don't think you can do that anymore." She joked, gaining a laugh.

"Don't worry, it's nothing! The crystals would help somehow! We still have those right?" Ms. Martinez asked Madison, who nodded.

"I'm pretty sure we do. But, I think we both know

what we should use them for." They both agreed on one thing. What was it? To bring back the Epitomus people! To Earthland, though. Epitomus is kind of…

Gone.

"I don't think you can do that anymore." She joked, gaining a laugh.

"Don't worry, it's nothing! The crystals would help somehow! We still have those right?" Ms. Martinez asked Madison, who nodded.

"I'm pretty sure we do. But, I think we both know what we should use them for." They both agreed on one thing. What was it? To bring back the Epitomus people! To Earthland, though. Epitomus is kind of…

Gone.

BRICK OF SOUND

MADISON SIGHED, WALKING TO THE ARENA. THE battle was going to start sooner or later, and she really just wanted to sleep. Some energy different from the King's evil was around her, and it was simply unsettling. It came off of Mandy.

Flashback Begins

"Really? You sure?" Chloe asked her, while Madison was upside down in her chair.

"Of course. I wouldn't lie to my bro. There's no way you wouldn't notice! I mean, you have enhanced senses!" Madison exclaimed. Chloe shook her head.

"It's like my senses are disabled here. Specifically in the arena. I wish I was better." Chloe looked away, until Madison patted her shoulder.

"You don't have to be better. You're still the coolest person I've known. Aside from Ms. Martinez, though." She attempted at reassuring, which still worked.

"Thanks, I'll remember that."

Flashback Ends

The tenor nervously fiddled around with her hands, reaching the end of the doorway. This was the second time she'd ever made it to the finals, and judging by how the last one went, it's going to change something.

"I hope I don't mess up in front of my friends. I was spared last time, since we got moved to a different area." She thought to herself. Madison stepped on the arena. Mandy was already waiting there, with her arms crossed.

"Ready to lose?" She questioned, already charging flames in her hands.

"No. Just make sure to go at full power!" Madison responded, trying to remain calm. The signal was given, so Madison moved to the side to dodge a double handed blast.

"You said full power, right? I'll go from the start! 500% Blaze!" Mandy shouted, the flames arising from the ground up in a swirl. Energy from it alone created a medium sized crater beneath her. It only covered half of her body, the right side.

"There's one thing you forgot about me!" Madison ran towards her. Mandy easily dodged her punch, and Madison looked her right in the eye before activating Drive 2. This intimidated her, since it was superiority glow. Mandy was caught off guard by a kick to the back.

"That you're annoying? Nope. I'll never forget!" She tried to kick her, but Madison caught her leg and threw her up into the air.

"She's also got good tactics." Ms. Stevens noted.

"All of my tacticians have flaws. Just wait." Ms. Martinez told her. Madison watched as Mandy began to activate her Tenor Turbo technique.

"What're you gonna do? Hit me with an attack?" Madison asked, obviously knowing the answer.

"500% Tenor Turbo!" Mandy came crashing down faster than she normally would. Taking that fear aspect into account, Madison kicked into something else. Black lightning. Right when Mandy's face got too close, Madison grabbed her and slammed her into the ground, going even deeper into the arena.

"If I take an attack, I know exactly how to counter it." The lightning turned back into steam, slowing down drastically. Opening her eyes from under the future tenor's hand, Mandy consecutively blasted Madison multiple times, until she stumbled away. Mandy got up, noticeably mad.

"This isn't a fair fight if you want me to go full power and you yourself aren't." She stated, confusing Madison.

"What? I am going full power! How stupid are you?"

"This tactician's weakness is obliviousness." Ms. Martinez explained. Mandy slowly walked towards Madison and picked her up by the collar.

"Your Dragon moves! That curse of yours! That lightning you just showed me!" She gave multiple examples.

"I don't know what you're talking about!" In response, Madison was kicked where her seal would be, but it wasn't there. She got herself out of arm's reach.

"I know exactly how to jog your memory." Mandy calmed down. Thinking this was a vantage point, Madison jumped into the air.

"Powerful Fist!" She used small blasts to create momentum to do as much damage as possible. Mandy began charging a blast, but lowered her hand when she got close.

The punch created a large explosion, sending gusts of wind throughout the arena.

"Unexpected." Bailey said.

"Don't worry, you'll get used to it." Chloe told the bass clarinet guard. Amidst the smoke, Madison repeated the same action that Mandy did to her not that long ago, this time with the other unconscious.

"You tricked me, didn't you! This was all on purpose! You used half of your power! Wake up!" She cried out, trying to get a response. Something in her mind was driving her insane.

"You told me to go all out, and I did! That doesn't mean you could just go back on your word! What's with you?!"

"It isn't supposed to be this way! Mighty-" Black lighting surrounded her fist, but she was interrupted by coughing. She coughed up blood, and was knocked out. When the steam cleared, it revealed both of them lying on the ground, with Mandy on the part with the broken arena.

"Looks like Madison won." Ms. Martinez teleported to the arena to pick her and Mandy up. While Mandy looked tired, Madison just looked…

Calm. Too peaceful, even. The only people who heard her freak out were the Mythical power users, with the addition of Ms. Martinez and Ms. Stevens.

"I need to regulate her power somehow with this break. It's going in multiple directions." Ms. Martinez thought, then picking the two up. She teleported Mandy to one of the rooms, and vanished to appear in the room Madison was in before.

"Brandon! Get over here!" As she said that, he broke down the door to get in.

"What is it?" He asked, walking over to Madison.

"Try using your frost energy on her." Brandon tried,

and succeeded. The energy was slowly healing her, and steadying her power flow. After a minute of focusing, Madison slowly opened her eyes.

"Where'd my master go?" Madison mumbled, starting to look around, until her eyes landed on Ms. Martinez.

"They died a while ago. Don't tell me you saw them." She said, as Madison wiped away a single tear.

"I did see them. They looked the same, and everything. But they smelt like potato salad." Madison remembered.

"That's plain out weird." He responded, walking out of the room by stepping over a door.

"You know you're going to fight me, right?" Ms. Martinez reminded her. Madison stood up, cracking her knuckles.

"Of course I know! I'm going to be the next number one!"

ONCE SHE RECOVERED, MADISON STRETCHED TO warm up. The king and the prince had left to their palace across the desert. This would be a battle without anyone important watching. Aside from the heroes, of course.

"So scary…" Madison said sarcastically, sat down on the floor. She looked at her bandages on her legs, remembering the moment. After her legs were burned, it permanently damaged her body and her mind. It was part of the reason why she always looked tired. She barely slept unless knocked unconscious by third party means.

"Are you ready yet?" Walter asked her from outside of the room. The tenor got up and walked out.

"Unfortunately. But, we've got to do this quick! There's a person we need to save!" Madison ran around, almost getting lost. She ended up at the arena somehow.

"It's the will to live, and there are different aspects.

Mine is specialized in evasion!" She caught one of the punches and flipped her around.

"She's still strong, even without her powers!" Madison thought, getting up off of the floor.

"You need to improve your base stats." Ms. Martinez told her, making the tenor clench her fists.

"I can't! My powers are barely able to reach my legs!" She shouted. Chloe knew about this secret.

Flashback Begins

"It's Madison time!" Madison exclaimed, attempting to bring out 345. Chloe focused to see how her power worked. The power surged starting in the core, and slowly made it throughout her body. It stopped right at her legs, though. Madison tried extremely hard to completely activate the form, but it went out, leaving her exhausted.

"Come on Section Leader, try it again! Just one more time!" Chloe attempted at encouraging her.

"I don't think I can do it one more time…" She panted. Madison could only activate it by chance now, and her body wasn't ready to take anymore, so she passed out.

"Bro!"

Flashback Ends

"We don't have to fight. We can just pack up now and start our journey." Ms. Martinez explained to the tenor, who coughed up blood yet again. Madison covered her mouth.

"Then who's the winner?" Ms. Martinez started walking away.

"Only the future hero, of course." She blandly said.

Oblivious to what that means, Madison just simply left the arena to find the spaceship.

"No clue who that is, but it's time to search!" Once she found the ship, Madison immediately changed into her hero outfit, this time with the worn down cape.

"I'm tired." Allie said, falling flat on the floor to the entrance of Madison's room. Madison was adjusting the tenor case strapped to her back.

"Not my problem. Go and do whatever." Madison walked out as the rest of everyone got into their respective bases to get ready. She sat the tenor case down outside of the spaceship, and noticed the sky. It was rapidly getting darker. Madison leaned against the wall, going on watch duty.

"Hey, loser. You know how we forget about things after we leave?" Mandy asked Madison.

"Why are you asking?" Mandy slammed her hands against the wall around Madison, who wasn't affected.

"So many things I can tell you now, but there's li-" Before she could finish, Allie ran outside.

"Madison! I pulled UR Tenor on Tenor Adventures!"

"Really? Show me!" The tenor followed her inside, leaving the oboe there. Mandy looked at Brandon, who was trying to destroy the trees with his Impact.

"What is it, traitor?" He had gloves on his hands that limited his strength output.

"There's one more thing I need to tell you."

BRICK OF SOUND

WHAT POWERS COULDN'T BE USED IN THE normal Darklands? Mainly flame like powers, unless you want to take the risk of burning yourself. Ms. Martinez was excused from this, due to being a Legendary. You're stronger in the Darklands if you have dark powers, which removes a lot of people from the list. Madison remains unaffected, since the color varies. Bailey is completely powerless, because her power is the opposite of the dark. Light.

"Good luck to you, 2.0!" Ms. Martinez stood in the same place, while Madison got in her fighting position.

"Same to you! Just make sure to fight fair!" Ms. Martinez took notice to this. So, when the match began, she used her superiority to erase both her and Madison's powers.

"Okay, the fight's fair now. Come on!" Ms. Martinez told Madison. Unable to use a blast (Prestige was erased also), she ran towards the hero. Ms. Martinez barely moved, and Madison almost fell out of the arena due to her clumsiness.

The ones that have different results are the 'control' powers. Walter's Time Control and Allie's Mind Control. The other member of the Big 3 also has a control power.

"Jeez, it's so dark, Bailey's practically invisible!" Madison joked. Only Kim laughed.

"You're right!" They laughed until they reached an invisible barrier. It had some text on it, but in a different language.

"It says 'Only those above the age of 100 may pass through.' I don't understand how you can't read it." Allie explained, gaining looks from the majority of the group.

"Alright then, my turn!" Madison ran through it, and succeeded at it too.

"Wow, you're very old." Mandy stated.

"Shut it. Alright, who's probably old?" Madison pondered for a bit, until she came up with a conclusion. She pointed over to Ms. Martinez and Ms. Stevens.

"Really? I'm old? What're you, ten?" Ms. Martinez asked, gaining a disappointed look from the latter.

"You're acting ten. Go and find out!" Ms. Stevens answered for Madison. Ms. Martinez, being mad that she got roasted, decided to test it out. It did indeed work, also for Ms. Stevens.

"So old, Ms. Martinez. I bet you're older than powers themselves." Madison said to the hero.

"You're older than powers themselves!" Ms. Martinez countered, as the barrier was replaced with a dome. It was a metal that was somehow see through. Despite the lack of technology, they had weird properties.

"Welcome to the Darklands Trials! There's five levels of darkness, and I'm at the final level!" The king announced. The system was similar to that of a video game. Beat up a villain, move up a level, rinse and repeat, right? Something was off, though.

"The rule is that Everytime you beat an enemy, I get stronger. Bye!" The king's voice went away, leaving the three there.

"Look, it's a dark thingy!" Madison looked to the center, and sure enough, darkness was spreading from a small cube in the middle. Before it could reach them, Ms. Martinez jumped in the air and blasted it from above. The darkness rapidly returned to the cube, and it began glowing.

"Commencing to Level Two." While they were fighting in the dome, the rest of the kids were on their way to the palace. Once they reached the building, Allie immediately kicked down the door. Oddly enough, there were no guards.

"Uh, guys..." Kim stumbled, turned around facing the back of the group.

"Now's not the time Kim!" Allie shouted back, beginning to walk inside.

"Allie. Look behind us." Walter told her, making Allie turn around angrily.

"What is i-" Behind the group was an army of floating instruments. They paused for a bit.

"Run for it!" Chloe exclaimed, and the group ran into the large building. They followed Chloe into a large room, seemingly the dining room. Inside was a large table, with too many chairs. At the very end of the chair was exactly who they were looking for.

"Oh, hello guys." They said to them, gaining multiple reactions.

"I knew you were the prince, James!" Allie responded.

"We can't know the prince's identity! We're gonna get banned from the royal guard, and I'm gonna be kicked out into the streets, and only make a dollar an hour!" Kim freaked out.

"Relax. We're leaving anyway."

"Guys, we're only in here because of those instruments that are outside! Don't you remember?" Kendall reminded them.

"Oh." Mandy and Brandon said in unison, despite having no reaction to the revelation.

"I don't see what the problem is with the instruments, it's not that hard to deal with them." James walked outside of the room, to see the instruments just floating there. As everyone watched in anticipation, he simply raised his right hand, and the instruments fell on command. They weren't harmed at all.

"Your weights are on, right?" Allie asked.

"None of us know how to take it off." He answered.

"While we're waiting, let's go and find the king!" Brandon shouted.

"Good idea for once. James, where's the king?" Mandy questioned him, while Kim was still freaking out.

"The control tower."

Minutes Later

The tower was large. It's unguarded, yet again, and had energy leaking out from the bottom. Darkness.

"The only way up is to climb." James stated.

"There's absolutely no way we can get up there!" Allie couldn't even see the top, as it was covered in clouds. Walter snapped his fingers, and the motorcycle appeared.

"If you get on, maybe we will." James used part of the ground beneath him to fly himself upwards. Brandon and Mandy jumped onto opposite sides to climb up it.

"You think you can beat me? I'll win by a landslide!"

Brandon was carrying Kendall on his back, who was nerfed severely by the Darklands Effect. Mandy was nerfed also, but was carrying Chloe.

"No you won't!" They raced each other up, only to be beaten by Allie and Walter on the motorcycle, who landed right in front of the door to the top.

"Looks like none of you guys won!" Allie yelled from above the clouds. Brandon and Mandy made it at the same time.

"Stupid brass." They said, looking at each other.

"Stop copying me!" Bailey and Kim were now guarding the tower.

"Those Earthlanders are weird." Bailey stated.

"You're right." James opened the door to the tower. Inside was a chair, with some monitors surrounding it. The king turned around in the chair, striking fear into the group.

"Just his presence is too much…!" Brandon thought, putting his hand over his mouth.

"What brings you here, Prince James? More guards?" He asked, still menacingly sitting down.

"We challenge you to a duel!" Allie spoke up. The darkness had no effect on her. More or less, it was just annoying.

"A duel? I haven't had one of those in years." The king stood up. He walked through the group, as if they weren't there. He stepped down the air like they were stairs until he reached the ground. Brandon and the rest of them effected stopped sweating bullets.

"He's way too strong. We can't even get close to him!" Chloe exclaimed, then being picked up by Mandy. Kendall was also picked up by her.

"Well, you can try!" Mandy threw the both of them like rockets towards the king. After screaming a lot, they landed on the ground right in front of him.

"You idiot! The darkness is going to get into their heads! Don't you remember they were villains?" Brandon reminded Mandy, who should've known.

"Oh, yeah. You're right." Brandon grabbed Mandy's arm and threw her over to the king as a distraction. Right when he dodged, Brandon appeared and punched him in the face.

"That tickled." The king simply touched his hand, and darkness overcame Brandon.

"Let's see how I can get rid of this." He thought, as the aura swelled around him. He tried dropping his body temperature drastically. It was originally 32 degrees Fahrenheit, so he dropped it to 0. The aura turned blue as he got over it.

"Looks like your ice brain can do something!" Mandy couldn't fight with her power, so as of then, it was just Brandon able to do something.

"Shut u-" He was interrupted by the Big 3 crashing down into the ground between the king and him.

"Old man, it's time for your resign as king!" Allie told him.

"Alright, kids. You can try it, but you won't succeed." As the fight started, Madison had defeated the 4th level of darkness.

"That took a while!" Madison exclaimed, falling to the ground. She wasn't exactly exhausted, but standing in the background wasn't what she was used to.

"Come on, clarinet man! Face me!" Ms. Martinez called out, becoming impatient.

"Yeah, face us!" Ms. Stevens continued. Despite their powers being polar opposites, Ms. Martinez being Sun and Ms. Stevens being Moon, they still are as equally competitive.

Quick info dump. Well known powers are given epithets, and a thing such as power compatibility exists. Sun and Moon have both had 9 users, so whoever gets the 10th will be the last. Power has only had 5, supposedly being passed down. Power's epithet is 'Incompatible Powerhouse'.

"I guess we're just stuck here." Madison said, looking around the dome. It was rather empty, aside from the lack of people.

"You just can't trust villains these days." Ms. Martinez sighed, sitting down.

"You're not supposed to trust them in general. What have you been doing all of your life, living under a rock?" Ms. Stevens asked her, repeating the action.

"Living with kids. Every day, something different happens. One day they're mad at each other for a game, and another day they're fighting over whose section is better." She answered.

"But the low reed section really is the best!" Madison added on, somehow balancing the tenor on her head.

"Okay, that's a great conversation starter. Random fact about this place, did you know I've been here before?" Ms. Martinez questioned the two of them.

"Yes, you've brought it up multiple times." They said at the same time.

"The thing is, I made it out alive. My mentor who went before me, on the other hand, he hasn't been back since."

IT DIDN'T TAKE LONG FOR THE DARKLANDS KING TO BE pushed back ever so slightly. That still was classified as an accomplishment to the Big 3.

"You've moved a centimeter. Isn't that cool? We're strong enough to move a king a centimeter!" Allie pointed out, high fiving Walter before going back to attacking. James was sending in rock after rock. Anytime the King attempted to fight back, Walter froze him in time for a small amount.

"Pretty formidable, especially for how young you guys are. I haven't gone even a tenth of my power yet, though." He broke the time control using sheer will power. His darkness began pouring out. James put his hand in front of the two brass, standing off against the King.

"Stay back guys, I know the full length of his power." James said, as the darkness began burning the grass slowly.

"Sure you want to do this, Prince James? We haven't fought since the royal induction." The king mentioned.

"If it's for the safety of my actual friends, not random guards, then yes." He blasted fire towards him. The Darklands king raised a wall of darkness to absorb it. To negate the darkness, he shot wind at it, blowing it away in the process.

"Are you sure we don't need to step in?" Walter asked to make sure. James looked back to them.

"Until I've dropped dead, you can just watch. We haven't seen each other since the Hero Exams." He responded, glancing back at the King. He swatted away a blast of Darkness.

"Hey, you're right! You said you left on a personal mission and never came back!" Allie remembered.

"I can't tell if you're angry or excited." Walter stated, with his hands now in his pockets.

"Well, now you know where I was." James jumped out of the way of a ground attack, landing in front of the tower.

"Don't do it." Bailey whisper shouted over to him, as he grabbed hold of the tower.

"What're you doing? Put that down!" The king shouted to him, as he picked it up with ease.

"Say goodbye to suffering!" James tossed it into the sky, completely leaving eye view in some seconds. The building of the tower took some time, but that didn't matter to him. He just wanted to get him mad.

"Once you leave the Darklands, you're no longer prince. You'll just be a distant memory to the kingdom. There will be a new and stronger heir to the throne than you'll ever be!" The anger in his voice became slowly more prevalent throughout each sentence.

"Oh, I wonder who this person will be? Possibly even a princess?" Allie thought out loud, imagining what they would look like.

"Hope they'd be a good fighting buddy." Walter said.

CHAPTER 19: ORIGIN OF THE MARTINEZ

"Is that all you'd think about?" Allie asked him.

"Yes, cause I'm not a weirdo like you." Back in the dome, Ms. Martinez began explaining her life story.

"Alright, once upon a time, there was me. Powerless Martinez!"

Flashback Begins

Ms. Martinez grew up similar to Madison, but with the addition of parents. Madison never knew hers. But she had a mentor earlier than Madison. The 8th user of the Sun Legendary, known as Number 0 or the Underground Hero, Mr. Shine!

"You seem like a good holder for my power. What do you say to having it?" Mr. Shine told the younger Ms. Martinez.

"Of course!" She trained and trained for a year. Right when she received it, it seemed like it was meant for her. Not long after she got it, she got both her Hero and Professional Hero License, gaining a perfect score on both.

Little did she know; the Number 0 Hero had a rival. An old friend of some sort. Mr. Shine had constant battles against the future king. They were friendly sparring matches, until the instrument war began. Around the time the Number 1 hero disappeared, that's when the King rose to power, and slowly went through corruption.

Since the world, or better yet, the universe couldn't function without a number 1, Mr. Shine became Number 1 for a short time. During this time, Ms. Martinez adopted a child. Who was this child, you may ask?

"What's a kid doing out here in the wilderness?" Ms. Martinez asked them, who shrugged.

"Nowhere else for me to go. And before you ask, no,

I don't have a name." They answered. The hero went to shake their hand.

"Well, maybe I'll call you…" She trailed off, thinking of names. What would be the perfect name to suit them?

"How does Allie sound?" Allie reached to grab her hand.

"Okay." Aside from hero work, Ms. Martinez now had to deal with a child. While raising and training Allie, Mr. Shine travelled to the Darklands to speak with the king.

"You're not the same as you used to be. Those instruments you were fighting may have had a negative impact on you, but that doesn't mean you should subject yourself to them!" He told the king.

"You come into my dimension, my land, my kingdom, my throne room to tell me what to do? Who do you think you are?" He shouted back.

"The number one hero!" They fought for about 10 days nonstop. The battle was so intense, it was the reason the sky was so dark. The king's darkness was so strong, it permanently altered the time of day. The fight wasn't in Mr. Shine's favor, due to him slowly losing his power after giving it to Ms. Martinez. So, he lost the battle, and shortly after, his life.

"Hmm, Stevens, wouldn't you say the air's different today?" Ms. Martinez asked Ms. Stevens, who was sitting down next to her.

"Yeah, almost like the sun's died down, even a little." They never discovered him, because right when Ms. Martinez went to the Darklands, she suffered an injury and had to go back. Mr. Shines body had haunted one of the instruments, but it disappeared. No one knew where it went, so people suspected it went to one of the other dimensions. People with Legendaries have free will, even if he lost it after the battle.

"Well, it doesn't matter if even the sun died. I'd still

follow you, as a hero and as a friend." Ms. Stevens told Ms. Martinez. She knew the reason why the sun lost a small amount of light. Ms. Martinez didn't, however.

"Thanks, I guess." And so, when Ms. Martinez rose to power, school soon started after. On her first day, she got lost, but ended up right in time to save a child in danger.

"No evil doers are allowed to destroy the band room!" Ms. Martinez called out from inside the flames. She shot through it at high speeds and managed to blast Chloe in the face.

"Finally, you're here." Mandy stated, gaining a look from Ms. Martinez, who landed on the ground. Her footwork for a legendary power was amazing.

"Hey, there's two of you!" She pointed at Madison and Mandy. They looked at each other, then back at her. After saving Madison, she trained her to fight the villains. Once they were retrieved, Ms. Martinez hosted a tournament. This was the tournament where in the finals Madison had gotten burned severely, leaving her bandaged up for a month. Ms. Martinez stopped by to give her various gifts or to just talk to her. This was while the band house was getting built.

"You're the number one hero, right? Go out there and fight villains or something!" Madison told her from under the bandages.

"Don't feel like it. Besides, I have other people cover up for it. Not like they need me out there." Ms. Martinez responded.

"Come on, you're The Martinez! You have to fight, or else you're going to gradually lose notoriety!"

"Would you rather fight them in your condition?" Madison paused.

"I can't feel my legs."

"Exactly. I have to make sure you heal properly. That blast destroyed your healing process, so I'm here to stop you from breaking windows." Ms. Martinez explained.

"I haven't broken a window ever in my life."

"Too bad."

Flashback Ends

Ms. Martinez sighed, getting up off of the floor. Madison looked up at her, wondering what was on her mind.

"I can't believe that you've gone through that much. My fault for not doing my research." Madison said, laying on the floor.

"You can't be at fault for something not related to you. It's fine." Ms. Martinez reassured her. Madison frowned a bit, showing the smallest bit of emotion.

"Everything has been going wrong. That's at least how it feels to me. You were supposed to die a while ago, according to Epitomus Madison. I think it's my fault."

"No, it's not. You gotta keep your head up high, tenor! Use those rocky moments in your life as stepping stones to your victory!" Ms. Martinez encouraged her. Madison got up to stand.

"That's the best thing you've ever said to me! Alright, I'm ready to fight! But how do we get out?" Madison wondered, looking around the dome. No sight of escape anywhere.

"With patience." Ms. Stevens stated. Not too long after, the dome vanished. This was the same time that James threw the tower out into space.

"Of course that works. You probably planned that." Ms. Martinez retaliated, crossing her arms.

"Nope, you're just bad at this kind of stuff. Besides, there's a king we got to fight!"

ASIDE FROM WALTER, WHAT WERE THE REST OF the Kelli Squad doing? They were sneaking through the kingdom. Along with Kim, who ran away from the fight.

"There's civilians, sure. But I can sense something else." Kelli said, scanning the area through her goggles. Her one-word attack was Sight. It basically gives her the ability to see anything, which is enabled by the goggles.

"It's the instruments!" Kim shouted from behind them. They turned around, and sure enough, there was a group of instruments. Mainly the ones that weren't clarinets. Saxophones, flutes, other brass and such.

"Let's see, who has the perfect power for this?" Kelli looked at each member of her group. She picked Enza, who stood tall against the floating instruments.

"Sorry, but it's for the greater good! Shell-and-Mortar!" Using both of her hands, she set off a close-up explosion of fireworks. Even though they were mostly stars, once it disappeared, so did the instruments.

"Dang, that was over doing it." Kandi told Enza, as there was smoke coming off her hands.

"You probably rank really high on your hero tests, with all of that explosive power!" Kim said to her.

"If being in top 15 counts, then sure! But we've got other things to do! To the graveyard!" It wasn't that far from the part of the kingdom they were in. This was one of their mini missions. It was a town rumor that anyone who went to the graveyard would get knocked out mysteriously.

"I can't sense anything here." Kelli stated, looking around the foggy area. Kim attempted looking around also.

"Obviously the rumors are fake. The citizens spread lies because that's the only thing they can do. Just dr-" Before she could finish, she was hit swiftly at the back of the head. She had strong durability, despite being powerless.

"This is starting to creep me out." Aaliyah said, slowly backing away.

"Agreed, maybe we should leave." Kandi responded. Kelli began picking up a signal, throwing water bullets at whatever it was. It was either too fast, or Kelli's reaction speed wasn't fast enough. Kim tried catching them as well. All she did was grab at the air, and she caught them.

"Oh, hello. How're you doing this..." Kim trailed off. It wasn't night or morning.

"I'm doing fine. Maybe we could talk about this if you let me go." They responded. Kim did so.

"Kim, we can't just let them go! We discovered a mystery!" Kelli whispered over to her.

"I didn't catch your name. Mind giving it to me?" She asked, as they jumped onto a building in front of her with ease. They turned back to look at her.

"It's Rayven. You can find me in the city of gold."

Rayven answered, then disappearing.

"Aaliyah! I've scored twice this week! I win!" Kim told the bass clarinet, who was about to run away.

"Fine." Aaliyah handed Kim a gold coin. She gladly took it, putting it in her pocket.

Deeper In The Forest

There's always someone that somehow ends up where everyone is.

There's always the outlier.

A figure was sitting on a rock in front of a stone, in gold, which presumably had something major on it.

"So there's two of them. Alright. A twin, maybe? They must've made a copy of them. Really early on, too. Someone is changing either memories or time itself." They thought, writing it down in a journal. A cloak was covering whatever outfit they had under it pretty well, but there was only a mask that covered their face. Their hair was visible, only leaving people with that to guess on who they were. The journal itself wasn't that long, looking to be for a report to last almost a year.

"…Maybe there's even two changing."
In the desert, James was holding off the king fairly well. Only because he knew his fighting style. If he didn't, he would've been dead. But it was also a plus that the king wouldn't dare kill his heir.

"Give up. If I went even at 30%, this wouldn't go so well." The Darklands king told James, who didn't care. His ulterior motive was to stall until Ms. Martinez showed up.

"Do it then." He responded. On command, the king began charging a large ball of darkness in one hand.

"If you insist, fallen prince." He threw it at him.

James noted that it was fast, so he intended to block it. Ms. Martinez appeared in front of him, absorbing the blast with her hand.

"Heh, my power is stronger than yours. Get ready for this fight!" She turned the darkness into sun energy and blasted it back. It was strong enough to leave a few burn marks.

"Oh, you're right. I guess your legendary powers get stronger the more it gets passed down. I'll go 100%, then." The king told Ms. Martinez, who tapped her foot impatiently.

"Hurry and fight me!" Ms. Martinez blasted herself towards the king, attempting at a Madison like attack. Her goal in this attack was to grab him by the shoulder and blast the king with all she had. He dodged the attack. Ms. Martinez blasted herself backwards to kick him in the side of his head, knocking him into a mountain.

"Go get em', mom!" Allie exclaimed to her, as Madison and Ms. Stevens arrived on the scene. Madison spotted the smoke coming out of the mountain.

"Did I miss it? Darn it!" Chloe grabbed the tenor's hand.

"I'll show you it later."

"Alright! This calls for The Martinez!" She generated energy at the bottom of her feet and shot off, in the direction of the mountain. The Darklands King released a huge amount of energy, leveling the mountains and those around it. Ms. Martinez jumped across each leveled floor, then punching the king.

"If only your master was here to see this!" He mocked. The comment angered Ms. Martinez, who charged a large blast in both of her hands. Once it was released, it sent off five separate blasts, getting larger until the final one. The power was so extreme that it sent shockwaves back where the majority of the group were. The wind travelled all the way to the city.

"I think it's getting serious over there! Let's go!" Kelli said to everyone, as they began running to follow her.

"There's no time for cheesy named attacks. If this is where my final battle is going to be, then so be it!" Ms. Martinez called out, walking towards the king, who was barely getting up off of the ground. Every step left a small crater in the ground.

"She's serious." Madison muttered, raising her arms in front of her to guard herself from the oncoming wind. When it calmed down, Ms. Martinez bolted towards the king at the speed of light. She jumped over him, turning around to punch him with all she had into the ground.

"I shouldn't have done that...!" Ms. Martinez thought, backing up a bit, as steam rapidly raised. She covered her mouth, as blood slowly came out.

"You're right." The Darklands King got up, darkness spreading from out of his body. Ms. Martinez backed up enough, until she fell, grabbing hold of the ledge. But then, half of the darkness was pushed back to the otherside of the mountain, as a figure appeared. Ms. Martinez looked up at them, almost passing out.

"Stevens...?" Ms. Stevens extended her hand to grab Ms. Martinez's, lifting her back up on her feet.

"If you're going down, I'm going down with you. Together," She began, giving some of her energy to Ms. Martinez.

"As the sun and moon."

Chapter 21

REALIZATION

"**G**LAD YOU WERE HERE TO HELP ME." Ms. Martinez was back to her senses. After that punch, she was closer to death. But, energy transfer works better with opposite powers for some odd reason.

"We've got to finish this fight. Star Toss!" Ms. Stevens clutched Ms. Martinez's hand hard, then throwing her at the Darklands King. She gained control of the momentum to kick him across the face, sending them both crashing into yet again another mountain.

"So epic!" Madison commentated, watching the battle ensue. The King emerged out of the mountain, being followed in hot pursuit by Ms. Martinez. The fight carried into the air. Energy released by both of them were mixing together in a spiral, as they circled each other.

"Your reign ends here! You won't see the end of this day!" Ms. Martinez shouted, throwing a fist. It was caught, then countered. She used her other hand to block it. "You know what, that's exactly what he said before he-" Ms. Stevens came in, blasting him from below.

"Don't listen to him! Keep your mind on the fight!" The Darklands King surrounded himself in darkness, using it as some form of armor. It solidified over his king outfit.

"That's his unbreakable armor. No one has ever broken it before." James stated.

"At least his unbreakable armor isn't as redundant as Brandon's." Mandy said, as Brandon got in her face.

"What was that?" He asked angrily. Mandy responded with the same expression.

"You heard me." The Kelli Squad and Kim finally arrived on the scene. The king began charging a small concentrated blast with both of his hands together.

"This is the end of the Sun!" He shouted at Ms. Martinez, who nodded towards Ms. Stevens. They joined hands.

"No, it's the beginning of a new era!" Ms. Martinez retaliated, as the blast came towards the two. They surrounded themselves with an aura shield, moving through the blast to land the final hit.

"Galaxy Finale!" They both exclaimed, combining their energy to break through the armor. It made a single crack.

"Do it, guys!" Most of the group called out, excluding the obvious ones. After a few seconds of suspense, the armor was broken through. The Darklands King was sent flying out of the atmosphere, and with no trace left. The duo landed on the ground.

"See, you can't do anything without me." Ms. Stevens joked, making the number hero cross their arms.

"What are you talking about? I could've won on my own!" Ms. Martinez countered.

"That was a funny joke, Ms. Martinez." Madison told

her, walking up to her.

"Yes, it was. Wait, that wasn't a joke!" Ms. Martinez responded, as the tenor laughed.

"Well, aside from that, it's time for the honorary mini celebration arc!" Ms. Stevens interjected, gaining approval from Madison.

"Yeah!"

"What are they talking about?" Ms. Martinez thought, then coughing. The steam started pouring out again. She fell, being caught by Ms. Stevens.

"There can't be a party without you. Come on!"

"Fine, you're right."

Kelli Squad Base - An hour later

Madison was drinking a glass of water, surprisingly not eating anything. She might eat something small, but after the curse seal was put forcefully on her, she barely ate anything.

"Hey, give me my food back!" Brandon exclaimed, throwing a chair at Mandy. She kicked it in half while eating with a fork and knife.

"No!" Mandy countered, grabbing a stray plate and tossing it at him. Brandon caught it with one finger and gently placed it on the table.

"Cut it out, you reeds! Enjoy the time you have left in the Darklands." Ms. Martinez told the two. Brandon walked outside.

"Wait, idiot!" Mandy followed him to wherever he was going. Madison put her glass down, looking around.

"So, how are the kids?" She asked Ms. Martinez.

"What kids?" She dead panned, gaining a gasp from Allie.

"You literally named me!"

"Oh. Sorry, it's been like, what, a century?" She tried remembering.

"Just stop talking. I thought you said you weren't old." Ms. Stevens said.

"No." Ms. Martinez responded. Chloe propped her feet up in a chair, falling asleep. She basically trained hard for nothing, so sleep would be somewhat rewarding.

"Kim, have you gotten any stronger?" Bailey questioned her.

"Nope. Maybe if I had a power, i-" She cut herself off, bringing more attention than wanted.

"I used to be powerless, so that's something we have in common!" Madison offered a high five, then receiving one. Powerless people are usually hard to find. As in being completely powerless. There is some powerless people who trained so hard to technically have a power.

"Heh." Allie chuckled smugly.

"Shut up." Walter said to her. Madison looked at her now empty glass, thinking of random ideas. Attack ideas, defensive ideas, joke ideas. That's until she stumbled upon a thought.

"Wait a minute, guys. There's something that I just realized." She said, standing up.

"What is it, 2.0? Don't tell me it's something stupid." Ms. Martinez asked, as Madison shook her head, looking down at her hands.

"When we save the world, it doesn't really affect the world around us. Everything we've ever done to save our dimension, nothing is different. It's like, uh…" Madison tried to say something significant, but trailed off, immediately diffusing the tension.

"The reason for that is the government cover ups. When big events happen that stop the end of the world, they give other reasonings. The citizens don't know what's actually behind the scenes." Ms. Stevens answered.

"I know what you're trying to say! It's like an ice cube!" Enza brought up.

"Please elaborate." Allie responded.

"Well, when an ice cube melts, it's significant to the floor, but not to the rest of the place!"

"Bingo! That's exactly what I was thinking about!" Madison sat back down.

"What a serious analogy for a serious topic. When I was taken by Epitomus Allie, the world around us didn't care. It was because the government said I went on a mission to Epitomus!" Ms. Martinez told them.

"There's got to be a reason for that. But, as far as we know, it's a mystery."

In a ruined city

A figure was sitting on a rock, lost in thought. Behind them, on the ground, was Epitomus Allie.

"Stupid kids, thinking they could challenge me. That's why you're dead!" The figure thought angrily.

In the Mysterious Forest

Brandon cleared out the trees with his impacts, leaving it as a small wasteland. He looked at Mandy.

"You're a traitor. If it weren't for you, this tourney would've gone fine. You've even gotten weaker, and I can't stand it anymore...!" He clenched his fists tightly, even making his hands bleed.

"I did it to get stronger. I want to become better than everyone, to become number one. That means being stronger than you!" Mandy shouted.

"You think you need a fake villain to help you gain power? What happened to you at the Band Festival? You were considered to be the strongest, better than me! Now you're weaker than the Big 3, who are at 50%!" Brandon shouted back. He has a point. Allie, Walter, and James do in fact improve, but it's at such a slow rate, that it's barely noticeable. All Mandy's power did was decline. For scale, let's bring in a power ranking chart.

If Ms. Martinez was a 10 at full strength, the Big 3 were at a 7 at 100%, all 3 respectively, putting them at 3.5 at 50%. Madison was at 3 at that time, Mandy and Brandon being 4.5. Brandon moved up to 5, while Mandy moved down to 3.

"What have you ever done to get stronger? You may have trained with your body, but not your mind. Your anger gets the best of y-" Mandy was caught off by a punch to the face, knocking her into a nearby tree.

"Shut your mouth! You did us wrong! Epitomus Allie can now control any of us! Because of you messing us all up!" The leftover ice was melted off by her flames, so she got up.

"Fine, we'll settle this the hard way!" Mandy charged towards him, dodging or blocking any punches he threw at her, so Brandon simply froze her arms. After countless battles prior to this, they had memorized each other's fighting styles. He used the ice to kick himself into the air.

"Bari Barrade!" He said in his thoughts, but all he did in real time was yell. He used ice shards to send towards her consecutively. They all missed, and Brandon landed on the ground.

"What is he planning…?" Mandy thought to herself, watching him hold up his hand.

"Say goodbye to that evil, and me." He began walking off, then clutching his fist. The shards exploded, making a decent sized crater. If he was going to make an exit, it had to have his impact.

In the Kelli Squad Base

Madison walked out, looking for some escape from any possible conflict. Of course, this had the opposite effect, leading her into a fight.

"Cloaked person, what are you doing here in this forest? I mean, it does fit the category for the Mysterious Forest." Madison asked, then mumbled to herself. The figure raised a hand, charging a blast.

"To end your story here." They answered, firing it. Madison dodged it, and the blast left a large trail of destruction in its way. Trees were leveled. Mountains were leveled. Until it stopped, it leveled everything in its way.

"Come on, let's try for one success!" Madison thought, before being slammed into the ground hard. They lifted her up by one hand.

"You're that weak now? You should be stronger by now! Or are you being hindered by something? Perhaps someone?" Madison laughed in their face.

"Haha, you said perhaps." After this remark, they blasted her in the stomach, sending her flying back to where she started, in front of the Kelli Squad Base.

While this was going on, Ms. Martinez was drinking some water. The water tasted horrible. When she looked down to see what it was, the water was in fact black.

"Stevens! This water is bad!" She shouted, gaining the attention of the mentioned.

"I didn't make it! Why are you mad at me?" Ms. Stevens retaliated.

"...good point. Hey, where's 2.0?" Ms. Martinez

questioned, then gaining the answer from a loud explosion outside. She slammed open the door, immediately picking her up. Madison had a hole where her curse mark used to be, as steam came out of her mouth. She opened her eyes.

"Where's the tenors?"

ORIGIN OF THE IMPACT

Since Madison's recovery speed had increased, the hole was mysteriously closed after blue steam showed up. Now, there was a scar there, just in the front. Madison didn't feel bad physically. She felt bad mentally.

"I can't believe I lost to a person I never met before. I really do suck." Madison thought, sitting down on the floor in her room. Her bandages went over her clothing, and the ones on her legs were still there. She looked up to a poster she had in the space ship. It was of Ms. Martinez, her most prominent inspiration.

"Why can't I be like her? She's just like, a ship of success! But, I'm a boat of failure." She glanced back down to the ground.

"Madison, we're going back tomorrow. If you want to go on any more trips, go now." Allie told her, walking into her room. Madison averted her gaze up to her.

"What exactly am I? Everyone else has these high up

backstories, but I don't have any." She asked. Allie crossed her arms, leaning against the door frame.

"Yours hasn't happened yet. Or you're just a different case. No use in being sad about it! Go and do something!" Allie answered.

"No, I can't. The scar is right where my energy core starts. I have to wait to rec-." Before she could finish, Allie picked her up and threw her into the wall, leaving a dent in it.

"Allie, quit throwing people!" Ms. Martinez called out from the living room. Allie walked out of Madison's room, leaving her to just slowly fall down back to the floor. While this was happening, Brandon was angrily stomping in the sand. Every time he was either in a direct confrontation with or even near Mandy, it triggered his competitiveness. In which, deep down, was actually anger.

Flashback Begins

At an early age, Brandon and Karla were both separated from their parents. They grew up in a forest, one of the few ones left after the Intense Industrialization Era. Sure, they did go to school. They both were somewhat good friends with Madison, who was powerless at the time. They lived off of stealing, going through the town and taking things. They had made a pretty good life in the forest.

Not every story has a happy end.

One day, a forest fire broke out, taking out tree one by one. Karla was out taking chocolate from a corner store, while Brandon was just chilling. He glanced out of the window, then widening his eyes at the sight. The fire was speeding through very fast, making him bolt out of the door. Once he made it far enough, he turned back to see what was there.

CHAPTER 22: ORIGIN OF THE IMPACT

The entire forest, engulfed in flames. All that they worked for, just gone. Brandon clenched his fists, looking up at the sky.

"Why the heck did this happen?" He shouted out, his voice enough to make a crater beneath him. This event awakened his power, True Strength. Brandon ran into the burning forest, dodging the trees as he went. Even though he traveled far, arriving at what was left of the house, he ran out of energy on the way. As he caught his breath, he was going to try and find what was left inside. But, he was stopped in his tracks.

A giant tree branch fell and struck him across the head. Brandon blacked out, almost falling. The fire suddenly vanished, being absorbed by one person. They grabbed him by his collar, then teleporting away.

"What's a kid doing in the forest?" The figure, now revealed as Ms. Martinez, asked, placing him down on the ground. She began healing him using the sun energy, which was way faster back then. Brandon soon woke back up, holding where the branch hit him.

"You know where that fire started? My place is gone now." He told Ms. Martinez, who shrugged.

"I couldn't sense anything weird or out of place. You know what, I can train you a bit if you want." Ms. Martinez responded. Brandon accepted, and for a few weeks, he practiced and reformed on this new ability. He learned his one named attack, which he called Impact. One day, paths crossed. Mandy was sitting in a room, reading through some sheet music. She had just become the tenor not that long ago, so it was practically mandatory. The door to the room was kicked down, with Brandon as the culprit.

"Hey, you! Tenor! You used to be a villain, right? Well, how are we supposed to trust you?" He asked, walking towards her.

"I don't know, how should I trust a hard head like you?" She countered.

"What was that?" Brandon asked angrily, kicking down the table, as the band binder landed perfectly fine on the ground. We don't condone binder abuse in this book.

The Tenor got up out of her chair, getting face to face with the Bari. They both reeled back to punch each other, landing a clean hit on the both of them. They stumbled back from each other.

"You aren't trust-able, since you use your gift from a hero like a villain!" He remembered that past event. Mandy walked past him, stepping over the door.

"That's something you don't need to worry about. One day, I'll knock some sense into you!" She declared, then walking away.

"Something...I don't need to worry about? I'll find that out one day, that 'Stupid Tenor!'" Due to the injury to his head, the memory was engraved in his mind. Just by the way Mandy used her powers, it triggers his anger from that moment before the branch hit.

Through most of his hero tests, he struck through them on pure brute force alone. With his power being considered heroic, as it was related to Power, any events including him weren't covered up. He was seen as a future pro, gaining invitations to multiple events and places. That was part of the reason of his departure when he got back to Earthland.

Brandon was invited to a hero school, which also had a band program, but was separate. He accepted, so Karla could also go into the hero program with him. Of course, he would also continue with the Bari. On his own impactful journey.

Flashback Ends

He stepped into the spaceship, walking through everyone to sit next to his Bari case.

"So, how was the walk?" Madison asked, upside down in a chair. Mandy hadn't returned in a bit, so this would be the perfect time to talk with him.

"Uneventful. I did come across a huge rock, though. It was about the same size as the High School Band Room." He answered, catching the future tenor's attention.

"That place is like the same size as the band house! Cool." Madison said. Allie, Walter, and James were discussing some things that were in the future.

"There's DHB, the Hero Exams, the next Band Festival, Carowinds, and finally, the decision." Walter listed off, also counting on his fingers.

"Five things that we have to go at 100% in. Maybe not Carowinds, since that's a few days we don't have to fight during." Allie responded.

"Hopefully." James added on, as the other two nodded.

"Those DHB kids, always talking about what's next. On that note, you lose." Chloe stated, placing a card down, defeating Kendall's SSR Bassoon.

"What? Impossible!" He exclaimed. Chloe held up the card. It was UR Bari X, the limited edition.

"Your cards are outdated. Make money off of those inventions, like that dragon, and maybe you could afford the new Shocking Speed deck! You know, that feature card is the best. LR Tenor." Chloe explained. The mechanic understood, putting his cards back into his deck holder.

"Alright kids, we'll be heading back to Earthland in an hour!" Ms. Martinez shouted.

"Okay." Madison said, walking back into her room. It was her favorite place to be in when crossing dimensions.

She began practicing her kicks, wanting to refine them before the year started again. A figure would be watching from a tree.

"I guess this one is the perfect candidate."

As THEY STEPPED FOOT ONTO EARTHLAND SOIL again, most of their memories had been wiped. Madison retained the most out of all of them, but forgot about the entire Darklands Tourney. All they could remember (with few exceptions) is that they went there and came back. But, completely foreign to everyone, were the addition of Bailey and Kim. When they arrived separately, close to the spaceship, they forgot about meeting them too, except for Madison.

It was like some sort of recurring reunion.

"Look, it's a bunch of weirdos." Bailey said, pointing towards Madison running out of the ship.

"At least they don't like kn-" Kim began, then being punched in the face by the former.

"Keep quiet! No bad impressions!" Madison ran up to them.

"Oh, hey guys! You're in Earthland now?" She questioned them. Kim nodded.

"Yup. We arrived here on different terms than you Earthland guys." She answered.

"But what about James?" Kim looked over to him, then gaining that same fear again.

"We can't know the identity of the prince!"

"Well, there's no rule on that anymore. Aside from government regulations, and how they're turning everything over to the Technological Era," Madison began.

"You're free. Free to make goals, make friends, relationships even. I know I won't be able to do that, though. You probably can." Bailey laughed.

"Probably? She stumbles over talking to almost anyone she finds of interest in the Darklands."

"Shut up! Now that I'm free, I can do things like that better! Just watch, I'll be able to get all of the women!" She exclaimed.

"Interesting ambition." Madison noted, writing it down in 'Orange Juice Recipes.'

"Wait a minute, did I say that out loud?" Madison patted her back comically, her notebook back in her backpack.

"Don't worry, the closet already closed."

"Are you serious? Now my plans have been foiled!" Kim shouted comically.

"What plans?" Bailey asked, completely confused to the situation. After about an hour, they got back to the band house. Madison was quick to go into the flute room, doing a review of her new notes. Brandon went into the Low Reed room to meditate, while Mandy stayed downstairs.

"So, what instrument do you play? We need another bass clarinet." Ms. Martinez asked Bailey, picking up a list of names. Of the new comers, the majority were of 7th graders. They wouldn't move into the band house until the 8th graders left for high school. But, they'd still join up with them for an event or two.

"Bass clari-"

"Perfect! What about you?" She then asked Kim.

"Clarinet." Ms. Martinez nodded. She reached out her hand to her

"The name was Kim, right?" She recalled, gaining a happy look from the clarinet.

"Yup." Ms. Martinez then thought about the possibilities after they shook hands. More clarinets? Possibly the ultimate low reed section, better than what it was esteemed to be? It was perfect! Five was a good number for them.

"By terms of progression, I'd say we're like our next generation of heroes! The Big 3, Chloe, Amy, and the rest of you guys." Ms. Martinez told them.

"There won't be another generation until you die." Amy said to her, gaining a laugh from the hero.

"Oh, really? Not what my master told me! He said that I can decide it."

"Yeah, with the wars. But that won't happen for like what, a year? We can train until then!" Allie exclaimed.

"Hope you guys are ready for the wars. It will decide everything from the beginning to the end. Whoever wins..." Ms. Martinez began.

"...wins the world. Maybe even Earthland as a whole."

"That's cool. Only one person wins the entire world?"

"If everything goes accordingly, yeah! It sometimes can be a battle to the death, but it all depends on the winner." Ms. Martinez described the war.

"But, due to the storyline, I can't talk about this for another book!" Ms. Martinez finished.

"What in the world are you talking about?" Amy asked. Upstairs, Madison was doing one handed push-ups.

"Come on, I've got to get to 100 this time! 97...98..."

She went to go to 99, but she slipped up and hit her head on the floor, falling over onto her back. Opening her eyes, Madison held up her clenched fist to the air.

"I can't get up...but I don't want to give up…!" Madison was out of breath, since she wasn't in the condition to be training. Mainly because of having a hole in her stomach for a few minutes. Steam came out of her hand, so she got up to see it closely. Madison's eyesight is bad.

"What the heck?" She looked at her hands, and they were releasing blue steam. Her power felt like it was draining, so she attempted at turning Drive 2 off. It worked half way. Sure, it seemed like it went away, but it was like her body was out of energy. Chloe opened the door a bit, glancing in.

"You good, Section Leader?" Chloe asked, as Madison looked over her shoulder.

"You could say that." She answered, falling again to pass out. Chloe caught her by the hand, and helped her up.

"Remember what you said to me that one time? 'I won't let you die!' Well, I won't let you either." She joked, making Madison laugh, while also coughing. Madison held both of Chloe's hands.

"I love you, Section Leader." She told her.

"I love you too."

"Section Leader, together, as Tenor and Bari, we'll shake the world! We'll both make it into DHB, and when I become the number one hero, you can be my sidekick!" Madison proclaimed, telling the past villain her dreams.

"Is that so? Well, you're going to have to live up to it, future number one. Let's get stronger together!" Chloe responded, raising her hand high. Madison high-fived her.

"Yeah!"

To PASS TIME, THE BAND DECIDED TO USE THE Legendary Crystals. Good idea? Of course. No one would notice the crystals unless they were sent right to them.

"Alright, time to summon them. Sun and Moon, join together with Power like how you have been forever!" Madison recited, as the crystals on the ground began glowing. They rose up to the sky, then giving off a red aura.

"Just hurry up and give me your wish so we can get this over." The voice said, gaining a small laugh from the Power user.

"So impatient. Anyway, can you bring back the dimension of Epitomus?"

"Nope. Dimension returns aren't possible." They interrupted.

"Dang, it's like it's some form of a store." Allie commented, watching Madison talk to the stones.

"Can you bring back the Epitomus people that fought against Epitomus Allie to this spot?"

"Sure. Bye." The crystals shot off in different directions, as the three people from Epitomus appeared. It was EP Madison, Mandy, and Chloe. EP Chloe hid behind EP Madison.

"Oh, come on. That place with the cl-" EP Madison began complaining, before being shut up by EP Mandy.

"Once we're out, we can't mention it anymore!" EP Madison nodded, then looking around.

"Huh, looks stupid. Is this Earthland?"

"At least we didn't have to get revived. Coming back comes at a cost, so go talk to Ms. Martinez about a mission." Allie told the three of them.

"A mission…? That sounds scary…" EP Chloe stumbled on saying, gaining a head pat from EP Madison.

"Don't worry, it's fine. Let's go!" They walked into the band house, leaving the two outside.

"They're the correct timeline, you know? Epitomus me is only two years older than me. Technically, bringing them back disrupts it." Madison stated.

"Who cares? Timeline's crap anyways. No point in dwelling on it." Allie responded, getting up off of the ground.

"We need to go find an old friend. Someone I learned a technique from. Can you fly?" Madison asked.

"Nope."

On a stray sky island

A person was roaming around the sky sanctuary, looking at the book that was on the altar. It was a book about all of the elemental rares. From Fire to Ice, Magma to Steam, Light to Dark, you name it. There were five pages detailing every single elemental power.

"Look, there she is! Hi Sarah!" Madison shouted over to the person, waving. Sarah waved back, as Madison landed with Allie holding onto her leg for dear life.

"Haven't seen you in a while! How's those legs of yours? Have they healed?" She asked, giving Madison a flash-back to what happened. Her expression dimmed a bit.

"You could say that! The Martinez said that it'll take at least a year to heal on its own." Sarah gave a high five to Madison, as Allie got off of Madison's leg.

"Who's this child?" Allie asked Madison, who began proudly stating,

"Of course, this is the wondrous Sarah, 3rd in power to the UVC! Secretly the strongest, because she has the technically 2nd strongest elemental power! The power of Wind, what surrounds us and what blows us away! In some cases." Madison whispered the last sentence, which was only picked up by Allie.

"Hey." She said somewhat angrily. Sarah laughed at the introduction, since it was in Madison's fan girl mode.

"Yes, she's correct. I'm the wandering wind hero, not necessarily a hero because I didn't join the course, but a hero because I saved a cat from a tree once!" Sarah told them.

"That reminds me! So, I have vague memories of this person that we fought some time ago…and I was wondering if you could help out?" Madison asked, reaching her hand out. Sarah accepted.

"With pleasure! It's nice to get a battle every once in a while! If they ever come back, I've got your back!" She rhymed, gaining a chuckle from the tenor. A rift opened up above them.

"Perfect! See you l-"

"Madison." Mandy said to her landing next to her on the sky island. She earned a look from her until Ms. Martinez followed suite.

"Is it important?" She questioned.

"Don't know, just followed her." Ms. Martinez answered, shrugging. Mandy went to embrace Madison, holding her tightly.

"I'm sorry for bringing you into my villain mess. I really hate going to sky islands, but I just had to say that."

"Come on, you're the oboe! You don't have to apologize!" Mandy tapped Madison's back, which made her begin floating, slowly upwards towards the rift.

"Ah- wait. Was this a trick?" She asked blandly, before shooting upwards towards the rift.

"2.0!" Ms. Martinez exclaimed, flying upwards to grab onto her. She wasn't fast enough however, due to her being overworked.

"Alright Mandy, that does it!" Allie shouted, going to punch her in the face.

"I had to." Mandy stated.

"What?" She questioned her.

"Epitomus Allie made me do it for a deal." Now wherever she was, Madison came crashing down into this unknown land, but managed to land safely. She began scanning the area.

"This is earth. But everything is-" She started, before seeing something. It was someone right in front of her, but lying on the ground, seemingly unconscious. Madison thought she had defended the opening until it had broken free.

"Hey! Wake up!"